# TRAVELER IN AN ANTIQUE LAND

Roger –
Very nice meeting you
at the 50th class
reunion. Best wishes.

Mike

MICHAEL FRONK
401 S. FIRST ST. #B6 B6
MPLS. MN. 55401

# TRAVELER
# IN AN ANTIQUE LAND

*By Michael Fronk*

Tasora

Tasora Books
5120 Cedar Lake Road
Minneapolis, MN 55416
(952) 345-4488

Distributed by Itasca Books
Printed in the U.S.A.

Interior design by Elizabeth Edwards

ISBN 10: 1-934690-44-9
ISBN 13: 978-1-934690-44-4

**To order additional copies of this book, please go to www.itascabooks.com**

# DEDICATION

*To Nita and my family,*
*whom I deeply cherish, as the source*
*of joy and meaning in my life.*

# PROLOGUE

*I met a traveler from an antique land*
*Who said: Two vast and trunkless legs of stone*
*Stand in the desert. ...And on the pedestal*
*These words appear: "My name is Ozymandias,*
*King of kings: Look on my works, ye Mighty,*
*And despair!" Nothing beside remains: round*
*The decay of that colossal wreck, boundless and*
*Bare, the lone and level sands stretch far away.*

*Percy Shelley*

*What if everything is an illusion and nothing exists?*
*In that case, I definitely overpaid for my carpet.*

*Woody Allen*

# CHAPTER ONE

**Thomas Traveler** was rewarded just for being Thomas Traveler.

The month was July, the year 2023, as Traveler made his way towards the Key West movie set. As an internationally famous journalist and a player at the highest levels of power, he lived in Washington, D.C., but was a peripatetic globe-trotter with assignments everywhere. This time, two Hollywood moguls-in-their-own-mind had sought him out to advise on their latest film.

In his late fifties, standing several inches over six feet, Traveler was remarkably fit. His two hundred and ten pound frame, almost unchanged from his football days at the University of Alabama, was a study in bold strokes—no delicate lines or subtle shading—and gave him a rugged, bearlike authority. A classic jutting chin completed the effect.

His only physical flaw was a slight limp, the result of a wound from the Bosnian war some thirty years earlier.

The fourth generation of a wealthy Southern family, he had been sent to Choate, graduated from Alabama, then served as a CIA operative in Bosnia. He had been wounded in an eastern Bosnian village in 1995. He had watched as two hundred Muslim men and boys were brutally murdered, and had been shot in the leg as he made a futile attempt to intervene.

His cane, and recurring nightmares and flashbacks were a constant reminder of the ordeal.

This experience and attendant anguish transformed him from an idealistic warrior, secure in his Christian faith, to a post-war drifter. After he was well enough to walk, he had left Bosnia, and spent the last part of that decade in aimless wandering, his family money bankrolling journeys around the world.

One evening in the late 1990s, he found himself on the streets of New York, and saw posters for a rally that night with evangelist Billy Graham at Madison Square Garden. On a whim, or perhaps propelled by nostalgia for the comforting certainty of his childhood faith, he ventured into the giant venue.

The blend of showmanship, patriotic intensity, and revivalist exhortation worked its magic. By the end of the rally, he, like so many others, was swept up in the mass fervor, moving forward with the throng to the front of the auditorium—where he accepted Jesus Christ as his personal savior.

But just as his cane had become a physical crutch, Traveler sometimes wondered if his born-again conversion had become a crutch of a different nature.

❖

With his family connections, his status as a grizzled war veteran, and his resurrected faith, Traveler then decided the time was right to transform his newfound—or refound—convictions into political opportunity. Supported by the best speechwriters and operatives money could buy, he won his first bid at elective office in 2002, elected to Congress from his home district in Alabama.

His youth, life story and charisma launched his reputation as a political phenomenon. Though he easily won a second term, his bible-thumping oratory fitting perfectly with his constituents' mores, the fruitless gridlock of Washington quickly soured him. So he had again reinvented himself—this time as a journalist.

He had had his first big break when he gained access to one of the era's pre-eminent politicians, also a born-again, and had written a series of articles that documented the man's struggles—in leading the nation into two wars and unprecedented financial deregulation and collapse.

After that, Traveler interviewed and wrote about a long list of notables and celebrities, from popular entertainers, to philanthropists, to sports superstars, to business tycoons—virtually anyone who was famous for something.

He had further burnished his credentials with a book-length memoir of his experience in Bosnia, received to great critical acclaim, and in the next fifteen or so years his career had continued to flourish.

His deep belief in evangelical Christianity was well known, and he practiced an almost-extinct form of "old school" journalism, treating his subjects with scrupulous respect. The political elite, especially his staunch co-religionists, came to trust him as one of their own. Even those who did not share his faith developed confidence in him as a fair-minded observer.

He knew most people would have been happy to have enjoyed a mere slice of this kind of success. But he had a nagging feeling that despite the adulation, and even his faith, perhaps he had long sought only fool's gold.

He yearned to know where his path would end—or even if he was on the right path at all.

Still, his reputation had certainly led him into numerous interesting byways; earlier that spring he had signed on for a short stint as a "consultant" with one of Hollywood's hottest studios. The movie industry was not what it had once been. Like everything else around the globe, it was in a state of decline.

What consulting expertise was expected of him remained unclear. But it made no difference to Traveler; the money was excellent—the brothers seemed to have an endless supply of cash—and a good story, perhaps even another award-winning book might come out of it.

As he walked towards the set, he was joined by the ever-attentive Savant. Savant was Traveler's on-again, off-again resident bartender, limo driver, and confidant. He also possessed a portfolio of various esoteric graduate degrees and a seemingly encyclopedic knowledge of just about everything.

"So what's on the agenda for today?" Savant asked, as Traveler greeted him with a quizzical smile.

"Don't know. They didn't say."

❖

The studio's directors were brothers and self-proclaimed geniuses, which manifested itself, among other ways, in an odd preoccupation with using foreign clichés. As Traveler approached, one of the brothers, in typical fashion, greeted him with, "*Que pasa*, man?"

The other brother quickly slipped out of his director's chair, and striding towards Traveler, extended his hand. Traveler was one of the rare people the brothers took seriously. After all, he'd been everywhere and knew everyone—at least everyone worth knowing.

The brothers' latest movie was nearing completion. Traveler had never pretended to grasp the essence of successful film-making, and the appeal of the brothers' current effort, *An Affair Too Old to Remember*, completely eluded him. He could only guess that it was perhaps but one more reflection of the human race fiddling as civilization went up in smoke.

The set buzzed with the usual assortment of cameras, electrical cords, lights of all sizes and intensities, and extras milling around; but what made this set different was an elaborate audiovisual network with two-way communication to a secure undisclosed location.

If there was one thing the brothers loathed, Traveler knew, it was film-making advice from amateurs, which they defined as anyone other than themselves. Only an unusual circumstance would have compelled them to embrace the presence of a consultant.

That circumstance was the man with the money.

Traveler had not been asked to the set to offer any artistic opinions, of course. This time the brothers needed help lubricating the relationship with their key financial backer—the Chairman.

In an atmosphere of universal decline and disaffection, the mysterious Chairman had managed to become one of the world's wealthiest individuals, his wealth allowing him to become one of the world's most reclusive individuals as well.

He reigned over a vast communications empire with tentacles in the Internet, mobile applications, TV, movies, radio, and what remained of newspapers, magazines, and book publishing. Whatever you read, listened to, or watched, the Chairman likely owned a piece, if not all of it.

He also had his pet projects. The brothers' latest movie was one of them, and as a control freak, the Chairman wanted to monitor everything to do with the making of the movie—which he did via the two-way hookup between the set and one of his many offices.

"The Chairman has asked to speak with you," one of the brothers said to Traveler.

"Do you know what about?"

"*Non alola sola*," said the brother. He was trying to say "I don't know" in Italian, but, predictably, had mangled the phrase.

"Bottom line, though," the brother continued, "he said it's urgent the two of you talk." Traveler parenthetically mused that "bottom line" was an odd choice of words, as making money had never seemed a priority for the brothers.

"Here's the phone number he wants you to call, at precisely eleven a.m. tomorrow morning, from your office in Washington. Cool with you?" the brother asked.

"Certainly," Traveler responded. "Before I leave, mind if I watch for awhile?"

"*No problemo*," the brother nodded distractedly.

Traveler wasn't sure why he was wasting his time. The movie offended so many of his Christian sensibilities. Maybe it was a subconscious instinct to audit the perplexing ways of *el Diablo*, as the brothers might put it.

The star was an actor in his sixties, who had been a fixture back when Hollywood was still semi-flourishing. He was one of those aging leading men you recognized but could never quite identify by name. He was familiar but not really famous, and as he rightly worried, familiarity over time had bred audience contempt. In the process, he had developed a peevishness that only an irredeemably second-rate actor could perfect.

The movie revolved around a pair of one-time lovers who meet again much later in life. The story, a black comedy of sorts, was ostensibly set in Venice, one of the few cities that still maintained a certain aura of romance.

The heroine, while on vacation in Venice, takes a gondola ride; recognizing one of the passengers as her partner in the long-ago fling, she taps him on the shoulder. Without actual introduction, it becomes clear that the "hero" only vaguely remembers who she is—thus the title, *An Affair Too Old to Remember.*

The affair itself had ended badly, at least for the heroine. Her lover had dumped her, and she has long harbored a simmering desire for revenge. When she meets her former flame, she can hardly believe her luck. Thus begins a delicious waltz of retribution.

After the gondola ride, the couple makes their way to a small café for afternoon espresso and pastries. The hero stumbles through a feigned recollection of their previous trysts. As they drain their last drops of espresso, they agree to meet again at his hotel.

The shooting schedule for the day was set to film the moment where the two stars are about to rendezvous at a Venetian hotel room. (Many scenes leading up to this moment still needed to be filmed, though in Venice, California, not Venice, Italy. As the brothers saw it, "The magic of paint, a few two-by-fours, electronic enhancement, and Mexican stand-ins will do the trick. After all, those ethnic types look pretty much alike.")

❖

The scene was now about to be played out. The heroine had informed her once-upon-a time lover that she would be accompanied by a friend. Though no one specifically mentioned *ménage à trois*, the inference hung in the air.

To appear as the "friend," the heroine would use cosmetics, a hair color change, extravagant dress (vinyl head to toe), and the pretense of being French.

She had hired a female impersonator to represent herself, as the villain's declining eyesight had become as obvious as his declining memory.

Earlier in the filming, the aging star had expressed his doubts about the script. *An Affair Too Old to Remember* had numerous twists and turns, with an elaborate plot and set of subplots, but one element had troubled him from the beginning.

"I'm worried that the audience just won't accept that our leading lady is young enough to have been my paramour," he had confided to the brothers.

The only reason the brothers had not collapsed in hysterical laughter at this preposterous conquest of vanity over reality was that they lived so removed from reality themselves. "We understand and, *certainement*, we empathize," one said with an air of pained sympathy. "As you know, it's becoming almost impossible to find leading ladies who can match your preternatural youthfulness."

The brothers neglected to mention that their leading lady had voiced her own concerns. "Hey guys, give me a break," she had sighed one day. "No one will believe that old goat and I once had an affair. They'll think it's incest, for Christ's sake."

Instead, they reassured him, "Your leading lady, we know, is doing everything she can to enhance that vitality you always bring to the screen. Please, for her, for us, for the entire project—"

"All right, all right," he acquiesced. "I appreciate the pickle you're in. I'll persevere."

Since that initial blowup, production had proceeded without major incidents. Now, however, with a critical scene imminent, the star had insisted once again on airing his grievance.

"I really do worry about the reaction my public will have to this part of the story. You must remember that they are accustomed to seeing me—typecast, I might add—as vigorous and noble."

The brothers guessed that those theatergoers who might still identify themselves as his "public" numbered at most in the double digits. They were astute enough to understand that a broader audience perceived him as a typecast pompous buffoon, perfect to play an arrogant, bumbling philanderer.

The brothers saw their main job as preventing farce from descending into sloppy pathos.

❖

There was so much triviality and coarseness that occupied people's minds, Traveler again thought to himself. Broadly accepted religious faith was too often being replaced by such nonsense as *An Affair Too Old to Remember.*

Traveler looked at his watch; it was time to return to Washington. You didn't keep the Chairman waiting. Waving off-handedly to the brothers, he and Savant stepped into a limousine that would take them to the airport.

The next morning, back in Washington and preparing for his call to the Chairman, Traveler put his feet up on his desk, carefully raising his injured right leg, and glanced around his office. Photographs of important people covered every inch of wall and desk space.

His gaze settled on a picture from almost twenty years past, where he was standing arm-in-arm with one of America's more ignominious presidents—who had been the subject of his first interview. Protest signs originally in the background of the photograph had been airbrushed out, but Traveler remembered they had read, "Bring the troops home now." The grinning man with the clownish expression, however, had been no more than a string-pulled marionette.

Traveler's glance then rested on a family photo, taken during some apparently joyful event he could no longer recall. He appeared to be in his teenage years, so it must have been taken in the 1980s.

His family had initially made their money the same way most in the agricultural South had, from large plantations. Both his grandfather and great-grandfather had accumulated their assets, of course, on the backs of African slaves. Traveler had been raised not only on the gospel of the Lord, but also on the gospel of social Darwinism. Traveler's father, beaming in the photograph, with his arm around his son, had regarded himself as a skilled and shrewd survivor.

The world had so greatly changed since then. A relentless decay had taken hold, starting, of course, with the already destitute. Food and water shortages had aggravated civil unrest, with assault rifles, land mines, and grenade launchers flooding one poor region after another. A general lawlessness had provided fodder for totalitarian leaders, especially in Africa, parts of the Middle East, and Latin America.

Energy was scarcer, the climate warmer, and financial instability greater. Many once-proud nations had succumbed to the dislocations. In Saudi Arabia, where oil output was declining rapidly, young adults comprised half the population, with half of these unemployed; corruption was endemic. The situation in China was no better. Rural western China had fallen further and further behind the rest of the country, with Mao-era social and medical safety nets long abandoned. What had once been arguably one of the world's more egalitarian societies was now one of its most unequal, with escalating strife.

Compounding these conditions, periodic viral and antibiotic-resistant bacterial pandemics had reduced the global population by more than twenty percent.

By the 2020s, even in the U.S. life continued to become more difficult, with camps and shelters sprouting up like mushrooms after a rain. Similar to the Great Depression's hoovervilles, tent cities were everywhere, on overlooked parcels of state and federal land. Many had their collection of pierced young people and graybeards, homeless because of skyrocketing unemployment and rampant health problems.

Fewer and fewer citizens were immune and could say with confidence, "It can't happen to me." Nonetheless, denial, political hubris, and pandering had precluded even weak attempts at any of the bold changes necessary.

It was with these perilous circumstances as a backdrop that Traveler now called the number he had been given for the Chairman.

❖

"Yes, the Chairman, please. Thomas Traveler here. The Chairman has asked that I call him at this time."

"Certainly, sir, the Chairman is expecting your call. I'll put you through."

Traveler had no idea where his call was being received. The Chairman's location was always kept absolutely secret. He could be anywhere.

"Traveler, it's good to hear your voice. How were things in Gay West? Or is it Queer West?" The Chairman fancied himself a keen wit.

Traveler didn't approve of homosexuality, but neither did he condone gratuitous slurs; with almost anyone else he would have rebuked such offensive humor. He was accustomed to speaking his mind, but with the Chairman one needed to be exceptionally cautious.

"Just fine, just fine," he replied. "The movie is going well, don't you think?" Traveler knew the brothers would be interested in any feedback he could tease from the Chairman's byzantine cranial pathways.

Much of the power the Chairman held over people was anchored in his enigmatic, ruthless unpredictability.

"Well, Traveler, the movie perhaps goes too far. I had assumed titillation, not slapstick. Then again, the film's crudity may be more appealing to the great unwashed.

"I have another reason for wanting to chat with you, however," the Chairman continued. "It may take a while for me to explain what I have in mind."

"Take all the time you want," Traveler replied. You always gave the Chairman all the time he wanted.

"The current, rather sad state of mankind, as you know, fascinates me. We are complex switchboards into which plugs are inserted and removed," he said, invoking an antiquated comparison. Then, moving into the late twentieth century: "We are mainframes, nuclear power plants."

Even when you listened to the Chairman with the greatest care, you were always left wondering, *Is this visionary brilliance, or simple gibberish?*

"It takes a village, Traveler, and our village is under assault. We're losing." Traveler wasn't sure exactly what the Chairman thought was being lost. Normally he might have attempted levity: "Are you sure it just hasn't been misplaced?"

However, he only murmured, "Indeed, indeed," keeping his thoughts to himself.

"Yes, we're losing it, and we've got to get it back. I have a plan that requires your participation. I'd like to continue this conversation face to face. I want you to meet with me as soon as possible."

"Certainly." Traveler paused. "If only I knew, you know..." He was finding this awkward. "If I knew exactly where you were."

"Not to worry. I will have a car pick you up at two p.m. tomorrow afternoon, and then have you flown on a private jet out of Washington. Similar arrangements, if you like, will be made for your assistant."

"Yes, thank you, that would be excellent," Traveler said.

The Chairman's last words were, "Life is a journey. I want you to follow the path of the long march we are taking."

# CHAPTER TWO

**The following day**, as promised, Traveler and Savant were driven to Dulles airport and boarded a jet. They were about to embark on a circuitous route to their ultimate destination.

The six hours they spent flying directly west to Los Angeles passed quickly; after landing, they were whisked to a nameless port and in near darkness were led aboard some kind of watercraft, where they were attended to by a solicitous first mate before retiring to their separate cabins.

Late the next morning, they found themselves, refreshed by saltwater breezes, standing at the railing of a large yacht. "A vessel such as this," Savant said, "you could live on for months. A real beauty."

With his plethora of degrees, and an amazing memory, Savant knew the yacht they were on could take them anywhere, with a cruising range of about seven thousand nautical miles. At one time it had been a true luxury craft, with several decks, salon, private sun deck, library, and four spacious staterooms.

But even the super-rich, men like the Chairman, could no longer afford to maintain all their possessions in pristine condition. The yacht needed a bit of painting here, some polishing there. The normal crew of nine had been reduced to five.

"How far we going?" Savant asked his companion.

"How should I know?" Traveler replied gruffly.

Savant was accustomed to his boss's occasional brusqueness. Traveler adhered to the highest moral principles, but he could be short-tempered. Undaunted, Savant persisted. "So, boss, how much do we know about the Chairman?"

Traveler hesitated; then, growing more amicable, he said, "A lot of myth-making surrounds the Chairman. I've heard that enemies several years ago started discreetly referring to him as the 'albino'—because of the ghostly complexion he's developed by spending so much time in darkened rooms. He keeps the light out, apparently, to protect against skin cancer.

"It's also been said that he's a fanatic about germs, that everywhere he stays all the windows and other outlets to the larger world are sealed. But this may be just idle rumor. No one would dare to put anything in writing, even anonymously on the Internet."

The Chairman jealously guarded any details about his reclusive lifestyle, and with eyes and ears everywhere, anyone disseminating unfavorable information about him would risk an untimely demise.

Traveler now worried that he might have said too much. Standing silently on the foredeck, he grabbed the railing in lieu of his usual cane, and watched transfixed as a pair of dolphins raced alongside.

While Traveler was lost in contemplation, Savant noticed an inflatable rubber life raft tear loose from its mooring along the hull of the boat, and drop into the sea. Obviously damaged, it began to disappear slowly beneath the water's surface.

*A life preserver*, Savant thought, a trite symbol perhaps, but not dissimilar to Traveler's cane and fundamentalist beliefs. Savant hoped they would keep his companion afloat longer than the rubber raft he was watching sink out of sight.

After several hours lounging on the deck, the twosome watched the sun, which seemed to have been setting in a leisurely fashion, suddenly disappear below the horizon. As a purple glow settled in where the sea appeared to end in a perfect horizontal line, one of the crew approached and advised that cocktails and dinner would soon be served below deck.

Even by reduced standards, the dinner that evening was exquisite. Vintage wines were followed by selections from a full menu of appetizers and entrees. Traveler chose the baked Alaska for dessert, Savant the bananas Foster.

Savant, with his endlessly inquisitive mind, enjoyed the game of reading significance into the smallest details. Could baked "Alaska," for example, have any special meaning? He'd have to sleep on it.

After awakening, Traveler and Savant saw the silhouettes of freighters, anchored in port, coming into view. Soon they were stepping off the yacht, met by a pair of gentlemen in identical blue suits and identical dark glasses.

At first, Savant had whimsical hopes they were some kind of reincarnation of the Blues Brothers of *Saturday Night Live* fame, figures from another era.

They were, of course, the Chairman's minions, ready to escort them to an international airport about ten miles away. Traveler and Savant boarded an aircraft they learned would "take them north." (Aha, Savant thought to himself, the baked Alaska.)

Once airborne, Savant tried to return to the subject of the Chairman, but Traveler had closed his eyes. Savant always took this ritual to be an afternoon siesta, but Traveler referred to it as his "special time with the Lord."

The arrival "up north" was a carbon copy of their previous experience, as Blues Brothers clones again greeted the pair. This time they were taken to a railroad depot. Three cars had been reserved: a vista dome style coach for sightseeing, a second for dining, and a third with sleeping quarters.

Their route would traverse Alaska and some of the most mountainous scenery in the world. Perhaps, Traveler thought, this part of the journey would more closely reflect the Chairman's "long march."

"It's more spectacular in the Himalayas," said Traveler, as their train passed rugged outposts and melting glaciers, "and this is certainly less intriguing than my trip on the Orient Express in, I think it was about 2011."

Savant knew that in December, 2009, the Orient Express had, in fact, ceased to operate and the route had disappeared from European railway timetables. He took this as sufficient invitation, however, to make another learned observation.

"And during the train's heyday in the 1920s and 1930s… the scandalous company, the opulence, royalty, spies, an experiential feast!"

"Yes," said Traveler, as he shifted his large frame and scratched his chiseled chin, "then there was that time when a snowdrift stopped the train in its tracks, and a murder was committed during the night, an American, if I recall correctly, who was stabbed a dozen times in his compartment, with the door locked from the inside, no less."

Savant didn't point out that, yes, there had been a snowstorm in 1929 that prevented the Orient Express from moving for ten days, even though it was only sixty miles from Istanbul. No murder had taken place, though. All the passengers had survived nicely, with the help of local Turkish villagers.

Traveler was confusing history with the famous Agatha Christie mystery, *Murder on the Orient Express*—and little did he know that, despite his adventurous life up to this point, he would soon be involved in matters that even further blurred the line between fact and fiction.

❖

Traveler and Savant were soon aboard a second yacht that was even more impressive than the first.

Much about the Chairman's world was clearly paradoxical. He had conveyed a great sense of urgency in meeting with Traveler, and yet here Traveler was, crisscrossing the North American continent.

Standing alongside the captain as they moved out of sight of land, Savant asked, "How long is this vessel?" Then before the captain had a chance to speak, answered his own question. "About three hundred and twenty-five feet, if I'm not mistaken."

"Quite correct," the captain smiled scornfully. "Anything else you can tell me about my ship?"

Savant's intellectual intelligence greatly exceeded his emotional intelligence, so, missing the sarcasm, he responded eagerly.

"Actually, yes. I believe the Christina O was originally built in the early 1940s as a Canadian convoy escort, and was purchased by Aristotle Onassis in the 1950s." Raising his voice several decibels, he continued, "There are eighteen staterooms, each named after one of Onassis's favorite Greek islands."

"Can you name them?" the captain asked petulantly.

Traveler brought the discussion to a close, interrupting with, "By the way, Captain, my travel instructions neglected to indicate our final destination. Where are we heading?"

The captain replied only, "I'm sorry, sir, but the Chairman does not permit me to reveal that information."

For the next week, Savant and Traveler remained cocooned aboard the Christina O. They spent long days in restless reverie, anxious to conclude their lengthy journey.

The ambient temperature grew warmer each day, and occasionally Traveler and Savant began to glimpse palm-covered atolls in the distance. On the seventh day aboard ship, the captain announced, "You will be arriving at your ultimate destination tomorrow morning. The Christina O will anchor off shore, and a small boat will take you to a landing where a helicopter will transport you to the Chairman's compound. He has asked that before you leave I give you a brief description and history of the location.

"The Chairman's residence is situated on an island of about eighty square miles, thirty-five miles off the coast. It served as a prison until the early 1990s, when the Chairman purchased it. The island's volcanic mountain is almost always covered in clouds. Its security is not only supported by its isolation; strategically placed underground explosive devices are also a deterrent. There is only one residence, that of the Chairman."

The next morning, Traveler and Savant disembarked amid lush tropical greenery at the island's shoreline. A few dilapidated buildings were scattered about, but otherwise they could see little sign of human habitation. Suddenly a helicopter appeared and landed on a fragment of paved surface behind the buildings.

After boarding the aircraft, within a few minutes Traveler and Savant descended to a small heliport adjacent to the

Chairman's compound. Only the most trusted employees knew where to find it, as dense vegetation made the compound all but invisible from the air. For the world's super-rich, isolated enclaves and small private armies had become standard accoutrements.

A beautifully restored Rolls Royce met them at the landing strip. They were first driven to a resort-like complex, with a swimming pool and the other usual amenities. Savant proceeded to a reception area, from which he was then escorted to his room.

With Traveler now its only passenger, the Rolls drove another mile or two to the compound's main building. Here Traveler pulled out a sheet of paper from his shirt pocket. It was from the Chairman.

Traveler unfolded it and read, "Tell the driver to park on the left side of the road, forty-five feet from the entrance. Have him measure the distance exactly. He is instructed to always carry a tape measure. A second person will then approach your vehicle and provide directions as to how many steps you should take to get to the front door. If you do not take the precise number of steps indicated, you will be asked to repeat the procedure."

Traveler, emerging from the car with the help of his cane, followed the Chairman's instructions to the letter, and before long found himself in an ante-room to an ante-room to the Chairman's office.

He was met by a hum of activity, a beehive of phones, TV

sets attached to satellite dishes with U.S. and international channels operating, shortwave radios, faxes, at least a half-dozen computer server racks, and a crowd of people punching keyboards and watching screens. The modes of communication ran the gamut, including mid-twentieth century teletype machines and rotary telephones.

It seemed plausible there might even be carrier pigeons caged somewhere.

A young man stepped forward from this buzzing mass to welcome Traveler. "Sir, it's a great pleasure to meet you. The Chairman has been eagerly awaiting your arrival. I'll take you into the next office."

With that, they moved to the end of the large entry room, towards a door flanked by heavily armed guards so impassive they might have been carved in stone. Traveler had caught sight of similar personnel in red berets and green fatigues stationed about the compound grounds. They spoke only when spoken to, replying in broken English, heavily accented but from an indeterminate part of the world. He was certain many more were on the island, hidden from sight, with still others studying screens that fed from cameras no doubt scanning every square inch of the Chairman's residential fortress.

His escort punched in a code, and motioned Traveler to place his thumbprint on a small touchpad next to the door. As it slid open, Traveler stepped into a more serene environment. Members of the Chairman's paramilitary force were in evidence, but otherwise the room could have passed for any commercial firm's reception area. Even the requisite young, attractive female receptionist was there to greet the Chairman's guest. "It's a very great pleasure to have you join us, sir. We've all been preparing for your visit."

Adjacent to the reception room were several smaller office areas. A gentleman of medium height and build emerged from one, approached Traveler, and vigorously shook his hand. "Mr. Traveler, I'm one of the Chairman's personal assistants," he said by way of introduction. Traveler suspected that a small legion of assistants were in attendance, each as nondescript as this young man.

"Let me take you to the Chairman," the assistant said. He led Traveler to another door; after undergoing a second thumbprint-touchpad process, the door opened, and after Traveler had taken several steps forward, closed silently behind him. Traveler found himself suddenly plunged into almost total darkness.

For an instant, he was back on that Bosnia battlefield, his senses besieged with visions of flying body parts. The wailing of women and shrieks of tiny children eclipsed his current surroundings, but some part of him was still grounded in the present: in a darkened room, dimly illuminated by candlelight.

Struggling to regain his composure, he used his cane like a blind man to find a path forward. Indistinct sounds emanated from the shadows. As his eyes grew more accustomed to the dark, Traveler finally saw a large mass seated in a single mammoth chair, with a second empty chair facing it.

The mass, an enormous human presence, was wearing some kind of grotesque disguise, which Traveler finally recognized as the face of Alfred E. Neuman, the "What, Me Worry?" poster boy of *Mad*, the twentieth century satirical magazine.

# CHAPTER THREE

**"Thomas, how good** to have you with us," said a voice from behind the mask.

"Come join me. I imagine that you are curious about the mask I'm wearing." Curious was a huge understatement.

"The mask serves two purposes," the Chairman continued. "First, built into it is a state-of-the-art air filtration system, preventing any germs from entering my lungs. Second, I'm attempting to emulate the Greek god Proteus. You know, the one who could change his shape at will."

Traveler moved slowly forward. The large human mass made no effort to rise and greet him, so Traveler leaned his cane on the facing chair, and extended his hand.

The Chairman reciprocated with a fishy handshake. "Your bum leg," he said. "Football injury or war wound? I forget which."

Traveler took his seat. "Bosnia, actually," he replied. He could now see that heavy drapes had been drawn to prevent light from entering the room. Whatever other motive the Chairman might have for banishing virtually all sources of illumination, he had succeeded in imbuing his presence with a menacing mystique.

The Chairman spoke again. "May I offer you a refreshment?

You'll find a variety of liquids in the refrigerator behind you. Please, help yourself." Traveler rose from his chair, walked unsteadily the few steps to the refrigerator, and pulled out a bottle of soda.

"We last met about a dozen years ago, I believe. And you haven't changed a bit. As handsome as ever. In many ways, I envy you." Traveler doubted that very much, but before he could respond, the Chairman changed the subject.

"I've been busy of late exploring transcendental meditation, biofeedback, Zen, yoga, drugs, acupuncture. I've found that extending nighttime conditions to a full twenty-four hours each day has many benefits. The people who live the longest are farthest from the equator. Skin cancer has something to do with this, but I believe that a reduction in stimuli, especially of a visual nature, also dramatically increases one's existence.

"I intend to live forever. That is, to have my actual physical presence remain alive forever—not what you Christians call some metaphorical 'everlasting life.' No offense, of course."

"None taken," Traveler said, nodding gravely.

"I think of myself as a sitting Buddha. Consider that our species had its shortest lifespan when we were trimmest and most active, hunting and gathering. I have come to believe that inactivity and acquiring physical bulk are the royal road to happiness and longevity.

"But I would suspect that you do not agree with me on this point, my friend, as I must observe again that you look exceptionally fit, even in this light, many years younger than your true age."

Abruptly switching topics again, the Chairman now said, "That bottle of soda you've been drinking should have done its work, so I need you to step into an adjoining room and provide a urine sample to one of my medical associates. And, oh yes, a blood sample, as well. Not mixed together, of course," he chuckled.

"I think I've vastly improved my sense of humor, don't you?" the Chairman asked rhetorically, pushing a button on an adjacent console. A door opened, and a man in a white lab coat entered.

Beckoning to Traveler, he led him through another door, down a long corridor, and into what appeared to be a medical examining room. Handing Traveler a glass bottle, the doctor, if that is what he was, invited him to use the bathroom just off the examining room and provide a urine sample.

"Just leave it on the shelf next to the washbasin when you're done," he said. After Traveler finished, the physician informed him, "Next on the agenda is the blood specimen. We monitor the Chairman's blood regularly, and he asks visitors to do the same while they are his guests. He's always interested in the white blood cell counts, hemoglobin and hematocrit readings." After drawing a syringe full of Traveler's blood, the doctor escorted him back to the Chairman's sanctum.

"I think you'll be particularly interested in your sed rate," the Chairman began. "I've been able to keep mine well below eighty."

"Sed rate?" Traveler asked.

"Sedimentation rate, that indicates the speed with which red blood cells settle in a test tube. It's one of the tests most useful to a physician. I have a full-time staff of four physicians, one of whom you've just met: an internist, pathologist, psychopharmacologist, and a surgeon."

At this juncture the Chairman paused. "Traveler, why don't we call it quits for today? We can meet tomorrow afternoon and continue our discussion. Anyway, it's time for my twice-a-day enema. I have an individual whose sole responsibility is to administer it. Good day, my friend. See you tomorrow."

After a moment or two, Traveler realized that, as the Chairman would obviously not be leaving him, he would need to leave the Chairman. He rose from his chair, grabbed his cane, and followed an assistant who had soundlessly appeared through the same door he had entered. He was driven back to the resort complex where Savant had been left that morning.

His comrade was waiting for him as he walked through the front entrance. "Here's your room key," he said, handing it to Traveler. "You'll find your luggage there. I'm told dinner will be served in the dining room in about an hour." Traveler did not reply, and went straight to this room for a brief period of spiritual meditation.

❖

"So, how was your afternoon?" Traveler began at dinner that evening. Savant sensed that Traveler would reveal little about his visit with the Chairman, and took a healthy swig of an old and expensive wine, served in a fine crystal glass.

"A couple of the Chairman's paramilitary guys showed me around. I couldn't understand them too well. English certainly wasn't their first language. But I think they said the guns they carried were 'for the snakes.' Anyway, they sure enjoyed acting out the 'snakes' explanation part. We were in heavy brush the whole time, and the paths were narrow, and under constant attack from hanging vines."

Traveler held his glass of wine up to the light, as if looking for any signs of sedimentation. Savant went on.

"The bird life is magnificent. This must be one of the few remaining sites on the planet where you can walk through a virgin jungle and hear such a symphony of sounds. The trumpeting of majestic macaws, the wood instrument trills of multi-colored warblers, the toucan timpani. What an elegant fellow the toucan is, with—"

"Get on with it, Savant," Traveler interrupted.

"Well, we finally arrived at these wonderful white sand beaches, surrounded by palm trees of every variety, royal, the coconut, the date, the—" Traveler coughed.

"Well, you get the idea," Savant said. "I could tell the beach area and surrounding vegetation get constant care and attention. The coral reefs, of course, have fallen victim to warming waters and pollution, so there isn't much left. All in all, it was a satisfying day."

The pair finished eating in silence, which was fine with Savant. He was starving.

The following afternoon, after a leisurely and sumptuous brunch, Traveler found himself once again seated before the mountain of flesh that was the Chairman. With the darkness and the candles, the scene would have had a quasi-religious aura, were it not for the ever-present ludicrous mask. The Chairman took up his conversation from the day before.

"I have the most complete collection of Alfred E. Neuman memorabilia in the world. That's what the *Mad* people used to tell me. I like to wear a different Neuman air-filtration system each day. I believe the magazine did a terrific job for decades of presenting the critical issues of the time.

"The 'What, Me Worry?' kid became as famous as the *Playboy* bunny, while both publications were still in business. But let me tell you more about Alfred E. Neuman. What I particularly admire about him is his multi-faceted personality. He's protean..."

Perhaps sensing Traveler's uncertainty, the Chairman explained. "Like the Greek god I mentioned before, Proteus, very changeable. Proteus could take on whatever shape or form he wished."

Then with emphasis, "The contemporary world favors that kind of Darwinian adaptability, pretending to be all things to all people."

Although the Chairman's discourse contained elements of the absurd, sinister overtones were almost palpable. The Chairman's preoccupation with darkness, his secrecy, the obsessive concern with germs, blood tests, and uncomfortable medical procedures, his physical inertia, not to mention the somehow macabre masks—it was indeed menacing. One felt like a stranger lost in a Halloween night's fog.

"Alfred E. can be a real comedian," the Chairman continued. "*Mad* magazine thirty-three illustrated him as a jack-in-the-box on the cover. On cover fifty-six he campaigned against JFK, shown with a supporting cast of LBJ, Humphrey, Nixon. He was, like you, a crusading journalist on cover sixty-six." The Chairman was rattling the cover numbers off from memory.

"On cover eighty-six he transformed himself into Lawrence of Arabia, and then turned right around to become King Kong on cover ninety-four. He's a musician, an animal trainer, a big-game hunter, can walk on stilts, parachute out of planes. He was a gangster in the Bonnie and Clyde mold, and reemerged as a '60s flower child, a grand guru of Haight Ashbury.

"He enjoys cross-dressing, loves building sand castles, ski jumping, playing practical jokes, performing magic, eating pizza, boxing, fraternity parties, surfing, pissing in the snow, circus performing. He is a man for all seasons," the Chairman concluded, almost panting from his impromptu monologue.

Pausing for breath, he pushed another button on his console, and a portable sink emerged from the nearby cabinet, close enough so the Chairman need not move from his position. Running liquids over his hands, applying various lotions and creams, the Chairman spent the next few minutes cleansing himself.

"Perhaps we should continue our session another day," he said, as before ending the meeting on a capricious, arbitrary note. "Tomorrow I'll tell you the specific reason for bringing you here."

❖

On day three, Traveler sat across from the Chairman with barely controlled anticipation. But the Chairman's first words were a disappointment.

"The strawberry, not the apple, is really the most important fruit," he said. "The myth about the Garden of Eden is just flat-out wrong. What Adam and Eve were warned not to eat were strawberries, the true forbidden fruit."

Traveler desperately hoped this was leading somewhere. "Even the Beatles honored the special place reserved for the strawberry in their song, *Strawberry Fields Forever*."

Traveler surprised himself with, "That was from the *Magical Mystery Tour* album, wasn't it?"

"Bravo! Now here's where I need your help."

Traveler leaned forward in his chair.

"But first, I must give you some background."

Traveler slumped back in his chair.

"Hobbes had it right, you know," the Chairman said. "About life being short and brutish. The American people hunger for someone to lead them back to a promised land.

"I believe that Reverend Christian and Conman can provide that leadership, to launch a New Politics crusade, if you will."

Traveler was taken aback. Christian and Conman were both iconic public figures. Christian was the leader of a mega-church, university, and multi-media broadcasting empire, while Conman was perhaps America's most influential African-American spokesman.

Both were hugely forceful figures, but Traveler believed the pairing of the two men was completely implausible. Each possessed an immense gift for oratory, but in Traveler's mind they lacked political resonance with the general public. Even more, he wanted to know exactly how they would be compatible with what the Chairman was calling his New Politics agenda.

Traveler had heard vague rumors about some kind of third party the Chairman wanted to start, but its ideology was wispy. Rampant speculation questioned the Chairman's motives for setting up such a party. At the very least, surely it had to do with expanding his power.

The Chairman quickly continued, "The electorate's faith

in our political process, clearly bankrupt and beyond redemption, has reached a nadir of hopelessness. Now, launching the New Politics will not be easy. It will demand extraordinary planning, finesse, and the experience of only the most skilled individuals..." The Chairman left the sentence hanging. Then, "Will you help me?" he asked brusquely.

Traveler took several seconds to compose his thoughts.

"So what you are saying is that you believe we have reached another one of those genuine turning points in history."

"That is correct."

"That America's dissatisfaction with representative government has crossed a threshold, a point of no return."

"Right again."

"You sense, I believe, that the destruction of the old will not be difficult, but that the establishment of a successor, the New Politics, as you call it, will require Normandy-invasion-type planning and implementation precision."

The Chairman's pleasure was apparent. "Yes, Traveler, you've got it."

"Are you sure," Traveler said, "that I'm qualified to help you carry the banner for this effort? I'm honored, but—" The Chairman cut him off.

"As you would expect, I've given this matter a great deal of consideration. Every option has been thoroughly analyzed. I want you to be a key player in helping Reverend Christian and Conman become America's next president and vice president.

"These two men may, at face value, seem ill-suited to serve in the roles I've mentioned. That, counter-intuitively, is what will ultimately make them so appealing. We will be able to paint them as the quintessential outsiders, renegades, the independent thinkers America so desperately requires.

"The next election will be, as I've suggested, a tipping point. The tectonic plates are ready for a major shift, an upheaval. Things will never be the same afterwards."

The Chairman's values, as much as Traveler had ever been able to discern, were troubling and offensive. It was apparent that the Chairman had never made the slightest attempt to lead anything resembling a Christian life.

The Chairman might, in fact, be certifiably crazy, but his dreams for the future, at first blush, did have a certain sweeping grandeur. His assessment of the current political landscape seemed accurate. And he had the wealth, drive, and intelligence to make his vision a reality.

The question Traveler asked himself was what part, if any, he should play in the Chairman's scheme. Did he have a choice? Deciding that he did not, he acquiesced.

"What would you like me to do?"

"First, you and Conman have crossed paths over the years in your political and journalistic careers. He trusts you. I want you to become reacquainted with him. Gauge the depth of commitment you think he would bring to a project of this nature.

"The details of our mission will be clarified in good time. Even with the little I've told you, I know you'll figure out how best to present this to Conman. Once you have done that and reported back to me, you'll get your next assignment. Any questions?"

"I don't believe so," Traveler lied. He had many, but he sensed the conversation was over, so he rose from his chair, adding as he turned, "And, again, Chairman, thank you for this opportunity." Traveler hated hypocrisy in any form, but rare occasions required that it be practiced.

The Chairman, a huge, silent mountain of flesh sitting serenely behind a mask of Alfred E. Neuman, said nothing.

# CHAPTER FOUR

**As Traveler** left the Chairman's headquarters, he tried to take in the magnitude of what had happened the last several days.

As he invariably did in times of doubt, Traveler turned to his faith. It had helped him rejoin the human race, after the period of cynicism and despair into which he had sunk subsequent to the horror of Bosnia.

*Jesus will show me the way*, he avowed.

Traveler knew his first stop had to be Washington, to regroup and do some initial research. But before he could join Conman's entourage, he found himself swept up in an overwhelming, often bewildering series of events—that would have repercussions for him extending *far beyond their resolution*.

# CHAPTER FIVE

**The news of the explosion** at the Lincoln Memorial was on all the TV channels and all over the Internet, especially those media outlets controlled by the Chairman, which was most of them, of course.

Many had been injured by the explosion, some grievously; it was a marvel that only a single fatality had occurred.

The sole victim was one Joshua Jaffee. He was a familiar stooped figure at the D.C. central post office, an employee for the last ten years or so, and was easily recognized by the black velvet yarmulke he always wore.

As far as his small circle of acquaintances knew, the two idiosyncrasies that defined him were his passion for stamp collecting, and an abiding hostility toward those he called "foreigners." He was also known eleven hundred miles away, in Havana.

After the death of Fidel Castro, then his brother Raúl, relations between the U.S. and Cuba had normalized. Because Cuba was the location of the Palestinian embassy closest to the U.S., over the years Joshua Jaffee had sporadically chained himself to the embassy's front gate.

He would hold a large, handwritten sign, with a message that always urged the destruction of Hamas, Hezbollah, the Muslim Brotherhood, or some other Islamic organization.

For journalists, Jaffee's forlorn, bespectacled face and small frame chained to the Palestinian embassy gate had always been an irresistible photo opportunity. For a day or two, he would be famous.

And infamous to many of Washington D.C.'s Middle Eastern groups. Over time, international hostility between Christian and Muslim populations had ceased to be a festering wound seemingly beyond hope of rehabilitation.

In Iraq and Afghanistan, America had finally pulled out all of its troops, declaring "victory" in the face of interminable disorder. An Israeli and Palestinian two-state "solution" had been negotiated, and continued to hold, if tenuously.

Still, Muslims in Washington knew Jaffee all too well as a lone figure condemning the threat of Islam, real or perceived, demonstrating in front of local mosques and writing scathing letters-to-the-editor.

❖

So to many, what happened on that cloudless late summer day may have been surprising, but not inconceivable.

The U.S. postal system still functioned, albeit as a mere shadow of its former self, with delivery three days a week, if luck prevailed, and in the winter Joshua Jaffee rode the Metro to work, immersed in his beloved Torah. The Dupont Circle station was near his apartment, and the trip only took about fifteen minutes, perhaps twenty during the worst of rush hour.

The city's transportation network was badly in need of repair; as with most U.S. infrastructure projects, funding simply no longer existed, but the Metro managed to limp along.

During the summer, Jaffee rode his bicycle. As he pedaled along, he reviewed with pleasure the work ahead of him. He would do what he had done most days for the past ten years, ensuring the safe delivery of letters and parcels; routine busywork.

Reaching the post office, Jaffee locked his bicycle by the employee entrance in the back of the building. As he walked in the direction of his desk, he stopped momentarily at the commemorative stamp kiosk. He especially enjoyed studying the first-day issues, what stamp collectors called "panes," one hundred mint-condition stamps on a single sheet. Observing no new issues, he continued on.

He was always careful not to arrive early, which might force him into conversation with fellow employees. There was one unavoidable exception: a small, pudgy woman whom everyone facetiously called "Princess."

She had been given her nickname because of outrageous narcissism. In her late forties, likely a half-dozen years younger than Jaffee, she was in demeanor and behavior his antithesis. Where he dressed soberly, in muted grays, browns and blacks, she was known for her flamboyant style, favoring garish colors and lots of ruffles and frills; where he was reserved, she was gregarious.

"Top of the morning to you, Joshua," Princess greeted Jaffee boisterously as he passed her workstation.

"And to you, as well." Jaffee always reluctantly tried to maintain a certain civility.

"And happy birthday," she responded. Princess was a world-class busybody, and she seemed familiar with the details of everyone's personal history.

"So what did you do last night to celebrate? Reread the Torah for the umpteenth time? Rearrange your stamp collection?" But Jaffee was not without his own form of drollery.

"Oh, better than that. I reorganized my collection of Arab defamation materials."

Returning to a less controversial subject—she had never really understood his political views—she asked, "But how are your airmails shaping up?" Princess knew that U.S. airmail stamps were the pride and joy of Joshua Jaffee's collection. "What's their current market value?"

Jaffee grimaced. He had never fully comprehended his fondness for airmail stamps; it approached an addiction. Somehow the reasons for his obsession seemed rooted in his past, just beyond his conscious grasp, almost as if it were a passion belonging to someone else. Certainly, however, his love of stamps had nothing to do with money.

The day proceeded without incident, and, as usual, at the end of his shift, Jaffee took the mail and parcels from his personal mailbox, stuffed them into his backpack, and headed for the Mall. He received a fair amount of correspondence, most relating to his stamps, as he did business with a large number of fellow collectors.

His habit was to walk to the Lincoln Memorial, about ten minutes from the post office, and open his mail on a bench where he could see the huge statue of the great man.

On occasion, for reasons known only to her—certainly they were inexplicable to Jaffee—Princess forced her presence on him. She was often like a fly circling Jaffee's flypaper, as he found it impossible to avoid her buzzing closeness; this glorious afternoon was one of those times.

After securing his usual bench, Joshua sat, while Princess stepped away about thirty yards to smoke a cigarette. Jaffee took her temporary absence as an opportunity to enjoy his mail uninterrupted. Among his correspondence on this particular day was a sizable package. Perhaps he had received a birthday present.

As Jaffee took the box from his backpack, a group of tourists approached for a closer view of the Memorial. Though corroded by relentless air pollution, the Memorial remained one of America's most revered attractions.

The group was a mix of small children and aging adults, probably grandparents with their grandchildren. Two playful youngsters ran past Jaffee, momentarily distracting him as he started ripping the package's outer wrapping.

He had difficulty breaking through the brown paper, and the cumbersome box slipped from his grasp. Then, the bright day was made even brighter by a brilliant flash, followed by a deafening noise.

The package had exploded.

When the smoke cleared, Jaffee lay dead, thrown several feet from the bench by the force of the explosion, and surrounded by injured tourists. Soon, the blare of human distress was joined by whistles and sirens.

# CHAPTER SIX

**Detective Moab**, head of Washington, D.C.'s antiterrorism task force, was one of the first officials to arrive on the scene. Princess, catching sight of the detective, shouted amidst the smoke and debris, "I'm over here. I'm over here."

Moab—universally known by his first name, since his last name was a lengthy amalgam of unpronounceable Eastern European consonants—was not surprised to see her. He had known her since he had started out as a simple street cop, when his territory included the central post office; they had had a rumored liaison ever since.

He knew that she occasionally accompanied Jaffee to the Lincoln Memorial at about this time of day. For her part, she had immediately recognized him by his bald head and skulking gait, even amidst the chaos. Although he hadn't asked, or even thought about asking, she said, "I'm fine. Thank God you're here."

Pointing to where Jaffee had been, at the center of the devastation, she continued, "I think something blew up right in front of him." Then, the functions of the post office never far from her thoughts, "Holy cow," she said. "He just got..." she slammed her fist down as if clutching a rubber stamp "...cancelled."

❖

Traveler had arrived back in Washington alone; Savant stayed behind at the Chairman's compound to assist with the New Politics preparations.

He lived not far from the Lincoln Memorial, so when he heard the blast, he had naturally rushed to the scene, now a sea of blue uniforms and an ever-growing web of yellow police tape.

He found himself in the middle of a catastrophe which, by the perverse logic of his profession, had him captivated and energized.

Journalism was often a feast or famine business, and Traveler would soon realize he was about to feast in excess, to become a journalistic glutton for frightening ambiguity.

As he scanned the site, he quickly discovered that the carnage was more than he had emotionally bargained for. He felt a dreadful rush, almost like nausea, which he knew meant a flashback would soon be upon him.

*A whimpering lament, an orgy of grief—orgy of grief—orgy of grief...* Stumbling about, he slashed the air with his cane, as if somehow he could physically liberate himself from the psychological demons that beset him. He dropped to the ground, gasping for air as he tried to regain his equilibrium.

❖

No one noticed him in the general havoc, and after several minutes, his breathing returning to normal, he set forth to discover everything he could about Joshua Jaffee.

Out of the corner of his eye he saw a slightly overweight woman with frowsy blond hair; she seemed to be taking full advantage of her disaster witness celebrity, yelling and waving her arms histrionically.

As Traveler approached her, she intuitively perceived him as an official information gatherer. Before he could say a word, she announced, with an air of self-satisfaction, "They call me Princess," quickly adding as if to provide a key to solving the crime, "It's always the reclusive ones that get killed, isn't it?"

In response to Traveler's quizzical look, Princess launched into an explanation of Jaffee's routine, the walk, the opening of mail, the viewing of the memorial. She talked about the apartment he occupied in northwestern D.C., about the movies he sometimes discussed, and the occasional lady friend he might escort. Princess assured Traveler, however, that she was "absolutely positive" that any such relationships had never progressed beyond acquaintanceship, "if you know what I mean."

Traveler left as soon as he could extricate himself, and went off in search of additional background evidence.

As Princess watched him walk away, she reconsidered her previous observation. Maybe it was the reclusive ones who *committed* the crime—a dilemma that would trouble her for the remainder of the day.

❖

By twenty-first century atrocity standards, the Lincoln Memorial incident was unremarkable. It was, however, as the Chairman well knew, ripe for political exploitation.

Thus, he sent precise instructions to his media people, in the U.S. and beyond, on how they were to handle the story. Within hours of the event his media outlets had headlines screaming "Jew Assassinated in Nation's Capitol," and "Anti-Semitic Murder at Lincoln Memorial."

Given this kind of incendiary fear-mongering, the government could ill afford to be seen as sitting on its hands, so the next morning the FBI and the Washington police department held a joint press conference at the J. Edgar Hoover building.

At the front of the Hoover building's auditorium, two podiums occupied a stage that served as both a barrier and platform on which various officials crowded.

To convey the importance of the proceedings, the nation's attorney general was the spokesman, and stood before a microphone. He cleared his throat, and the noise from the assembled members of the media faded to a murmur.

The case would receive the highest possible priority, the attorney general assured those in attendance, as well as everyone who would be seeing the coverage later. He reviewed the facts of the case, and quickly closed with a few platitudes about national security. He did not take questions, and with pro forma grumbling, the news corps began scattering from the site.

Catching sight of Traveler in the crowd, the attorney general signaled for him to stay behind.

After the rest of the media had left the building, the attorney general instructed FBI and D.C. police brass to reconvene in one of the Hoover building's briefing rooms. Traveler was to attend as well.

The attorney general had been instructed to ensure this happened, but hadn't been told why; all he knew was that the president had been convinced that it was *essential* Traveler play a major role in the investigation.

Traveler waited as the room emptied, wondering about the who and why of his having been singled out. Not by the Almighty, of course. But then...

# CHAPTER SEVEN

**Police and FBI staff** had been working through the night to assemble background information on the homicide. In the briefing room, project lists and assignments, timelines, and preliminary suspects were written on large sheets of paper taped to the walls or scrawled on the available whiteboards.

Traveler glanced at the inventory of possible assailants: Middle Eastern assassin groups, Russian mobsters, American survivalists, white supremacists, black and Hispanic militants—a catalog of "malcontents." The attorney general strode to the front of the room and opened the meeting.

"Ladies and gentlemen, I need not stress again the urgent need to arrest the person or persons responsible for this crime," he said to the two dozen law enforcement leaders gathered in the room.

"Our president has promised to keep Americans safe. He will not permit this incident to go unpunished. The fact that such a criminal act could happen in the capital of the strongest military country on the planet—and in broad daylight, in front of the Great Emancipator, no less—is a slap in the face to all of us. It will not stand."

The rhetoric had all been scripted by executive order, but the president was only a conduit for the instructions; neither he nor his cronies were astute enough to have understood how this event could be turned to the administration's advantage. Someone else had devised the plan they were to subsequently follow.

"I want this initial meeting to be a brainstorming session where we get as much as possible out on the table," the attorney general continued. "By early next week I want to hold a second press conference, review the forensic information we have analyzed, and lay out how we'll be solving the case.

"So let's get started. Remember, there is nothing outside the bounds of relevancy here. Everything is grist for the mill."

"Islamic extremists, I would think, must be primary suspects," a first participant offered, without elaboration or justification. "I agree," a second voice chimed in. "After all, Mr. Jaffee was not only Jewish, but a known critic of Muslim activities." The Chairman's media slant seemed to have had its desired effect.

"I disagree," said Detective Moab. "If religiously motivated, the attackers would certainly have picked a higher profile target, like a synagogue or evangelical church."

The attorney general dismissed the suggestion with a disdainful wave; so much for "everything is grist for the mill." The attorney general wasn't the only one viewing Moab skeptically.

The detective had always been a bit of a curmudgeon, but in recent months he had become noticeably more erratic, subject to unaccountable fits of temper—and the whispers among his colleagues had reached the ears of Moab's superiors.

The attorney general now divided responsibilities among the federal and local authorities, and delegated point people for each task, with the stern admonition that he expected daily updates.

As the meeting broke up, the attorney general sought out Traveler. He suggested they walk along the Mall.

"Missed you at our last prayer breakfast," he said as they left the building. Like Traveler, he had become a born-again Christian. Unlike Traveler, however, his complacent Christian worldview never seemed to need reexamination.

"Yes, I've been preoccupied with other matters, out of the country for a considerable period of time. The life of the roving journalist, you know."

"Well, what do you make of this?"

Traveler chose his words carefully. "Creating effective procedures for conducting the case will be particularly important, I think. There are so many leads to follow." He kept his responses short and vague, knowing that the attorney general was a man whose loyalty was always in play.

It didn't take long for the attorney general to reveal the administration's agenda. "It appears that Mr. Jaffee was quite an Arab-hater," he said, then made his position brutally clear. "Constructing a case against Islamic terrorists shouldn't be that difficult. The president wants to send a strong message."

As political tides had always ebbed and flowed, lately the pendulum had swung back in support of ultra-conservatives. The national legislative torch had been passed to those who held views of an extreme persuasion.

"Traveler, the president wants you intimately involved in this investigation, and your assistant, Mr. Savant, as well. I will make certain that the full resources of the FBI and D.C. police force are at your disposal."

The two men had now reached the site of the crime. Some debris and a blackened circle at the epicenter of the blast remained.

As he gazed at the memorial from outside the yellow tape, the attorney general began to wax philosophical. "You know as well as the president and I do that this is part of what has been an endless struggle for the very soul of America.

"Of course, all we want is justice. That goes without saying. But the ends will justify our means. We must fortify our nation's faith in God."

The two men looked up at the granite presence of the man who had preserved the Union. The attorney general murmured, seemingly to himself as he began reading from the *Gettysburg Address*: "...this nation, under God, shall have a new birth of freedom..."

Turning, and staring directly at Traveler, he said, "We are pursuing the task Lincoln described much more than a century and a half ago. He dedicated himself to the same proposition to which we must dedicate ourselves, 'this nation, under God.'"

# CHAPTER EIGHT

**Traveler faced** a vexing predicament. It appeared that he had been asked by arguably the two most consequential men in the world to play a key role in two complicated assignments.

He would only learn much later how closely intertwined the two assignments were.

But since it would be a week before the next Lincoln Memorial investigative update, Traveler turned his attention to visiting Conman.

Conman, of course, had a real name, widely known to the public, but insiders and influence peddlers always referred to him simply as "Conman."

It was not necessarily used with derogatory connotations; it was more an acknowledgment of his natural talents. In fact, he was generally admired for his intelligence, shrewdness, and almost inexhaustible energy.

Well into his late forties, he was always in constant motion, like a spinning top. In his mind, frantic activity was the preferred alternative to concrete results. "It's the process, not the outcome, that I like to work," he had always said. And no one had worked the process better than Conman.

Although he had long ago made Chicago his home base, he could frequently be found in various cities in the U.S. and beyond. There was no place he didn't imagine as his opportunistic oyster.

This time, Traveler caught up with him in New York, where Conman was being well paid to give a speech to one of his favorite constituencies, Anglo-Saxon fat cats with some sense of civic guilt. Conman disingenuously made them feel moral and useful.

They were, as Conman would assure them, "part of a solution, not part of a problem." After a pep talk from Conman, they could return contentedly to their expensive homes in heavily guarded gated communities, where they ignored their children; or go to fancy hotel rooms, where they cheated on their wives; then to their opulent offices, where they cheated the IRS, their co-workers, and their customers. Conman was their father confessor.

"Fantastic to see you again, Thomas. It's been too, too long," said Conman, as Traveler walked into the suite where he was relaxing before the speech. He was surrounded, as always, by an entourage.

Despite Traveler's Christian values, which clearly conflicted with Conman's considerably more pliant ethics, the two were acquaintances of long standing.

"Yes, it has," Traveler replied to the effusive greeting.

"I understand you want to spend a few days with me to study the master at work, see if I've still got it," Conman laughed. Traveler waited for him to continue.

"Well, Traveler, old man, I think you'll see that I haven't lost a step." Conman was impeccably put together in an immaculate shirt and a finely tailored charcoal suit—London's best, with subtle white, yellow, and gray stripes. The yellow silk of his tie, subtly flecked with gray, was echoed in the handkerchief that winked from his breast pocket. Gold cufflinks and a thin gold watch completed the ensemble.

He stood, motioned to his retinue, and said, "It's show time." The group, Traveler with them, left the hotel and climbed into the stretch limos that had pulled up at the curb, amid the garbage which the city was picking up less and less frequently.

"It's getting harder, but I always try to travel first class, Traveler," said Conman. "Image is everything."

As they arrived at one of the few remaining private clubs in New York, Conman was met with the back-slapping, hand-shaking, and other gestures of goodwill predictably accorded him, as he made his way to the club's banquet room. He was announced to a rousing ovation; he waited imperiously for the audience to seat itself, and plunged into one of his well-honed stump speeches.

As Traveler listened to Conman's mellifluous tones, the marvelous cadences and pacing, the mesmerizing phrasing, he thought back to the time that Conman had permanently made his imprint on America's psyche. He had been a basketball star, and leveraged his athletic prowess into prosperous celebrity.

One evening changed Conman's destiny forever, and allowed him to carve out his position as an influential, perhaps *the* most influential spokesman for black Americans.

As now, Conman had been in New York on that fateful night. He had been walking alongside the man who had long reigned as the black community's guiding light, its savior. The two men were about to enter an Italian restaurant when a stranger stepped out in front of them, fired a pistol several times, and fled.

Conman managed to throw himself in front of the great man, to partially shield the assassin's target—for that is what everyone assumed it was, an assassination attempt. In doing so, Conman took the first bullet and suffered a wound to the shoulder. His companion was killed instantly by subsequent shots.

It was Conman's defining moment. He claimed to have seen the gunman just before he fired, and to have leaped towards his comrade guided by "pure instinct." The media made him an instant legend, and Conman inherited the mantle of African-American leadership.

The apparent assassination remained shrouded in mystery and controversy, however. A few journalists had intimated that it was more than plausible that the gunman, who was never found, was an expert shot and had carefully aimed so as to cause Conman minimal injury. The allegations always provoked a howl of protest among his supporters, who pointed to them as proof of the country's lingering racism.

As Traveler sat at the back of the room, he listened to Conman's hip phrases, and observed the sinuous body language that intrigued men and women alike.

Charm was Conman's essence. The touch, the proffered handshake, the instant mastery and constant use of first names, the steady gaze, full on, never wavering. The smile, a sweetly gorgeous thing he flashed like the asset it was, like a wad of cash.

It was the entire constellation of traits that seduced people. Giving a speech, Conman had always said, "is like sex. You're supposed to be exhausted when you're done."

And so he appeared, perspiring profusely, as he concluded his remarks, traveled the gauntlet of well-wishers that led to the exit, and stepped into the cool evening air. "Not bad, wouldn't you say, Thomas?" he asked rhetorically. The entourage dispersed, and Traveler agreed to accompany Conman the next morning on an early flight to Chicago.

Chicago was Conman's town. He had been born and raised there, and felt as if the source of his animal spirits emanated from the soil of the place. Thus it was that his empire was based in one of the city's old buildings on the South Side, where a plaque above the door read, "People of God Coalition." Cynics had nicknamed it the "Pot of Gold Coalition," the final destination for the money that flowed through a rainbow funnel.

"Now these are my people," Conman announced to Traveler, as the two of them walked through the front door of his headquarters. The People of God Coalition occupied all three floors, and there was electricity in the air, with activity everywhere. Once it became known that Conman had entered the building, however, the moving masses turned as if in unison and began a clapping, cheering reception. "*My* people," Conman purred.

People of God had three dwindling sources of income. First, of course, there were the state and federal minority program funds. Such programs had never regained the money-making status they had enjoyed in the 1970s, in the wake of the civil rights movement, and grew smaller with each passing decade. Conman's business enterprises still attracted considerable financing; all the major participants in his schemes, some legitimate, some perilously close to fraudulent, got a slice of the revenue.

Conman had long derived his greatest gut-level pleasure from his third equally diminishing source of income, what he called the "tithing of white corporate America." What others had sometimes called simple extortion no longer carried the same coercive clout it once had. Nonetheless, the purpose of the day's visit was to plan an assault on the latest tithing target. Conman took Traveler to his private office, with a corner view on the top floor. Three of Conman's closest advisors followed them in.

"Good morning, gentlemen," Conman intoned in a resonant baritone, as the participants organized themselves. He propped a perfectly polished pair of wingtips on his desk, settled back into the smoky-blue leather of his chair, and asked, "So tell me, what do we know about Boston Grocery?"

His assistants had been through the drill innumerable times. Now more quaint ceremony than genuine exercise for getting cash, it still provided Conman lingering amusement. The relevant information was produced: "Boston Grocery has more than thirty retail outlets within the Boston metropolitan area, with a twenty to twenty-five percent market share. The company, now in its third generation of family ownership, is fighting to maintain profitability."

"Jew, right?" Conman interjected. Traveler winced.

"Yes. The Goldsteins are still an influential Boston family."

"Goldsteins? Then it'll be more gold flowing from the Goldsteins to the Pot of Gold Coalition," Conman whooped merrily. The display of naked venality made Traveler angry and ashamed, yet he remained expressionless.

"So what's our complaint, what are we demanding, and what are we threatening if we don't get it?"

"The complaint is the usual," an assistant replied. "Blatant discrimination. Failure to hire black folks. We've staged our routine incidents, hiring a guy who applied unsuccessfully for a warehouse position, as he exploded in a tirade of profanity at the interview. We got a lady to apply for a cashier's position, who showed up reeking of alcohol, and was turned away as well."

Traveler had heard enough, and left the room and waited outside the building, intending to rejoin Conman after he had finished his session.

Unfazed by Traveler's abrupt departure, Conman continued, "And what's our demand?"

"Two hundred thousand dollars, plus the immediate hiring of a dozen black kids whom we designate, each given a 'no cause for termination' contract. It will help increase our leverage in Boston." Conman knew that one key to his influence was maintaining a strong grass-roots base, and doling out jobs was an essential component.

"And what do we threaten? The usual?"

"Yes, a consumer boycott of Boston Grocery's stores, implied disruption of shipments, fueling anti-Semitic sentiment."

"Well, everything seems to be in order," Conman concluded. "Do we have a meeting arranged with Boston Grocery's management?"

"Tomorrow, at their offices. Your schedule is clear. You fly out in the morning. It's all in motion."

Without another word, Conman got up, and taking a back stairway, he reached the sidewalk, where his favorite personal vehicle, a serviceable canary yellow 2009 Porsche, was waiting. Seeing Traveler cooling his heels, Conman simply said, "I understand you have a proposal you want to discuss. Assume you can join me in Boston; I'll be flying out tomorrow."

Traveler checked his calendar, pondered the time remaining

before he had to get back to the Lincoln Memorial assignment, and answered, "Sure." Conman stepped into his Porsche and sped away.

❖

"So what's the proposal?" Conman asked, turning towards Traveler. The two of them were settling into their first-class seats on the flight to Boston.

Traveler took another sip of coffee, and placed the half-filled cup on his tray. "I've been talking to the Chairman," he began.

Conman's eyes immediately narrowed, to focus more intently. The Chairman's name always had that effect.

"Anyway," Traveler continued, "he has a truly visionary, compelling idea for a new political party, and has asked that you play a major part."

Conman remained perfectly still, like a small rodent that had just heard the screech of a raptor overhead.

"You see, the Chairman has concluded that our political process has, once again, reached a crisis point. That politically we're paralyzed. He feels our two major parties, as their authority has swung back and forth over the last century, have completely exhausted themselves. He thinks that the next presidential race can be won by a new party, with a new agenda."

"Well, yes, I can see his point," Conman replied cautiously.

Traveler took another long sip from his cup. "Americans have been repeatedly assured that one administration after another would finally 'clean up Washington.' An endless series of broken promises have finally and completely extinguished the country's confidence in its public institutions."

"So what does the Chairman want me to do?" Conman asked.

Traveler cleared his throat and added another spoonful of sugar to his coffee, stirring it slowly before he spoke again. "He wants you, as a part of what he's calling his New Politics crusade, to be the party's vice presidential candidate in the coming 2024 election. He believes that the New Politics party must reach across all the traditional political, racial, and religious boundaries. It must embrace a new diversity."

Conman's business was, in fact, the "diversity business," a part of the "race industry." His agenda had always been hypocritical. The last thing he really wanted was for minorities to improve their lot in life. His power depended on keeping a large base impotent and relatively poor, so that he could continue to exploit their grievances.

But for Conman, alas, too many minority individuals had risen to positions of success; even, more than a decade before, had included the election of the country's first black president. The race industry was clearly in decline.

There was no denying that Conman needed to make a fresh start. Perhaps, he thought, the Chairman's proposal just might enable him to effect a phoenix-like transformation.

"Who will be the party's presidential candidate, and what

major strategy does the Chairman contemplate for gaining success?" Conman asked.

Traveler had been told to withhold any further information, so he simply said, "Let's talk more after the meeting with Boston Grocery."

"Great," said Conman, adding, "In the meantime, how about a champagne breakfast? Flight attendant!"

## CHAPTER NINE

**Boston Grocery's** headquarters were Spartan and functional. A receptionist escorted Conman into a small boardroom, where he was soon joined by the three top executives, president and CEO Saul Goldstein, plus two other Goldsteins; Boston Grocery was nothing if not a family business. The executives were a dour, furrowed-brow group, clearly cut from the same ethnic and cultural cloth.

At the last moment, Conman had decided it would perhaps be best if Traveler remained at their hotel, counseling him that he feared the meeting might become overly discordant.

Saul Goldstein began the session by asking, with obvious sarcasm, "So, to what do we owe the pleasure of your visit?"

"Saul, I'm sure you and your family," Conman said, sweeping his arm grandly towards the Goldsteins seated across from him, "understand the purpose of my visit. As you know, I confront racism wherever it rears its ugly head, as it has done here at Boston Grocery." He knew that the subject of racism touched a sensitive nerve in the elder Goldstein, who was the patriarch of a family that had itself often been the victim of bigotry.

Saul Goldstein arched an eyebrow; undeterred, Conman lumbered on, "I will use every ounce of energy I possess to fight against injustice. As you well know——"

Saul Goldstein's patience had expired. "What I well know is that you have never taken a single action from which you did not derive personal gain. You preach equality, express righteous indignation about a litany of mankind's unfortunate ills—all pure demagoguery. More importantly, though, you no longer inspire fear."

Conman had increasingly heard this dismissive rebuttal in recent years. Even more distressing was that he had found he had a declining inclination to respond. Goldstein's riff was a bit more eloquent than most, but Conman knew he was right.

"Thank you for your time, then," he said. "You have already been advised of my demands. My associates will be in touch with you. Good day."

❖

On the return flight to Chicago, Traveler was prepared to wait for the right moment to once again broach the Chairman's offer. But only a few minutes into the trip, Conman turned to him and said, "So, Thomas, tell me more about the Chairman's plans."

Traveler stared out the window. "Let me put it this way. I believe that it will involve a positive end, though perhaps achieved by questionable means. You know that I disapprove of many of your motives, but I admire your gift to persuade, and fervently pray you have, at bottom, a good heart."

Conman was no more enlightened than before. But his recent confrontation with Saul Goldstein had demonstrated not only his waning power, but his battle fatigue.

"I'm ready to make the leap, my friend," he said. "What would the Chairman have me do next?"

"Just hang tight. You will be given further instructions at the appropriate time."

# CHAPTER TEN

**Traveler returned** to Washington late Saturday. Sunday, he went to the Capitol Hill Baptist Church. The speaker was the Reverend Christian. The topical theme of his sermon was "America Under Attack."

Christian's base of operations was a mega-church just south of the Capitol. He regularly led services at the Capitol Hill Baptist Church to stay in touch with many of the congregation's political heavyweights.

Traveler sat in his pew, mulling over events of the past weeks: the convoluted trip to the Chairman's island compound; the surrealistic meeting with the Chairman himself; and the instructions to persuade Conman to run as the New Politics party's vice presidential candidate.

Now he would hear from the Chairman's choice for the New Politics party's standard-bearer. The reverend began on an even note, but his voice soon grew vehement. "We can no longer tolerate the weakening of our values. The decline of the extended family. Increases in juvenile crime, alcohol and drug abuse..."

❖

Raised in rural Alabama, Traveler was the product of generations of Southerners with an unshakable belief in scriptural literalism. His parents and grandparents had attended meetings where the most famous revivalists of the early twentieth century had preached. His father had even dabbled in more unconventional practices, like speaking in tongues, faith healing, and prophesying.

What Traveler was hearing this particular morning was not much different in many ways from what his forebears might have heard. It reflected a view of America as a once-moral country that had grown dissolute, consumed with materialism, sapped of courage, no longer able to resist the evils that assailed it.

Traveler had slipped away from his faith after Bosnia. But that fateful rally had returned him to the fold. Billy Graham had been an honest man, with good intentions. Christian, on the other hand, had a sort of squalid sheen. Maybe it was the nagging impression that he, unlike Graham, did not really believe what he was saying. God was simply coin of the realm for buying power. And try as he might, Traveler had never quite made the leap to blind ideologue.

Christian was winding up his sermon with a series of rhetorical questions, a shopworn technique. In a call-and-response, the congregation met each question with a rousing chorus of, "No. No. Never. Never," each one more impassioned than the last.

"Are you in favor of abortion?" Christian began.

"No. No. Never. Never."

"Should prayer be banned from the public schools?"

"No. No. Never. Never!"

"Should smut peddlers be allowed to sell pornographic materials to your children?"

"No. No! Never. Never!"

"Should schools hire known homosexuals?"

"No! No! Never. Never!"

"Do you approve of burning the American flag?"

"No! No! Never! Never!"

Traveler was one of the few to remain mute.

In the final prayer, most of the parishioners, welded into one organism by their collective abhorrence of their country's corruption, vowed to wage relentless war against the forces of iniquity aligned against them.

Traveler left the church in a foul mood. He had witnessed, he thought, a crude caricature of what it meant to be Christian. Traveler's fundamentalism was deeply ingrained, almost genetically so, but though generations of his family members might have celebrated the morning's rhetoric, he increasingly found himself seeking a more caring, tolerant Christianity that was exemplified by the life of Jesus himself.

Although Traveler had come to attend Sunday morning services more out of habit than enthusiasm, the Sunday evening men's group meeting promised more genuine and intimate spiritual nourishment. Given his unpredictable schedule, he only attended sporadically, but each time he hoped to strengthen his faith.

He nodded as he entered the meeting room, greeting fellow seekers as he made his way to his seat. He settled in with care, setting his cane alongside his chair. This session began with one of Traveler's "Brothers in Christ," as they called each other, voicing distress that culminated in the cry, "There is so much to be afraid of in our world."

Another brother quickly responded, "You must steel yourself to keep on going and trust in the Lord." Somehow, all such exhortation and encouragement that had been a source of spiritual sustenance for Traveler in the past, now sounded empty. The meeting droned on with little to engage him; he was preoccupied with his twin missions, and his mind drifted.

He was abruptly yanked out of his reverie when a brother turned to him. "You fought in Bosnia. You've been close to conflict," he said. "How do we win God's war?"

Traveler remained silent, for so long the silence became mildly disquieting. "I wish I knew," he said, finally.

Then, jerking his cane into the air, he continued. "You see this cane? It's a partial salvation for my physical impairment. Being born again has been a salvation for my emotional impairment—but of late I'm finding that pursuing the Christian life is raising as many questions as providing answers."

This time the silence that followed was distinctly uncomfortable.

# CHAPTER ELEVEN

**Monday morning**, the media convened at FBI headquarters for another case briefing. The attorney general began by reviewing the latest forensics information.

"There is now absolutely no doubt whatsoever that the package Joshua Jaffee was opening was the source of the explosion. We have confirmed that the explosive device was nitroglycerin detonator-activated. Still, no fingerprints or DNA."

He paused awkwardly, as if embarrassed by what he felt required to say next. "There is one new piece of evidence, however. We have uncovered amongst papers in the victim's desk at the post office what I guess you might call a poem."

A typed copy of the document appeared on a screen behind the attorney general. Though everyone in the crowd was at least rudimentarily literate, the attorney general felt obliged to read the words aloud:

*"An empty lot. Scrub brush blows in the cold wind. No sound.*
*Only the blowing of the cold, bitter wind. I'm an insect, to be stepped*
*On, my body crunched. My hairy arms and legs scattered about, in*
*The empty lot. I wish to be God. To tell people where they can get*
*on, And where they can get off. The howling mobs, the armies of the*
*Night, marching at my command, As a child, I envied the horses,*

*With their muscled strength. If only I could once again ride those Horses like the wind, to freedom. And obliterate the evil doers."*

The nature of both the language and content left the audience mystified, although an awkward guffaw here and there erupted.

"What do you make of the message?" a voice finally rang out.

"All I can tell you is that the words were composed of cut-up newspaper type, with Joshua Jaffee's name scribbled at the top. We can only assume it was written by Jaffee's attackers."

"You must be assembling a psychological profile," another voice speculated.

"Yes," the attorney general replied, "but we will be cautious how we interpret such profiling." He paused again; it was hard not to suspect it was deliberate, for dramatic effect. Then, promptly violating his own admonition, he said, "The writer is obviously expressing a profound desire for retribution." He continued down a slippery slope, greased by predetermined intention.

"Those people who sent this message say they want to lead 'howling mobs,' and 'obliterate the evil doers.'" Though the assembled crowd may not have consciously realized it, his use of "those people" set up a subtle dichotomy between "us," presumably the American people, and "them." His next pronouncement left little doubt about who he considered "them."

"Our experts have judged this to be the characteristic language of…" he paused again "…of jihad."

Traveler listened intently. The attorney general had evidently given up all pretense of an objective, "let the evidence lead us where it may" inquiry. "We believe that we have a solid direction in which to take our investigation," the attorney general continued, "and expect to quickly bring these foreign assailants to justice."

Traveler had been conflicted about the current president and his administration, who wore "morality" and "family values" on their sleeves. Now the attorney general was asking him to play a suspect role in a scheme with dubious purpose.

Traveler thought again of his quest to incorporate Christ's message of forgiveness into his own life. What he had seen of the world, beginning in Bosnia, and now, maybe with this assignment, was making that seem quixotic.

❖

That afternoon, Detective Moab and other police operatives gathered at D.C. police headquarters, a few blocks from the Hoover building. The meeting was chaired by the city's police superintendent. Although he had never served in the armed forces, he favored a military management style, where the leader decided what needed to be done, and told others to do it. "Team decision-making" was a completely alien concept.

"All right, men," the superintendent said. He was not technically correct, since the dozen or so individuals gathered before him included four women, but he was oblivious to such distinctions. "It seems pretty clear that this crime has its origin in the Middle East." He and the attorney general were obviously on the same page.

"What any good investigator seeks is grounds, original cause," the superintendent lectured. "The Lincoln Memorial bombing has religious fanaticism written all over it. First thing we do is interview Jaffee's landlady. She's Lebanese."

❖

Detective Moab, who had been restless since the session's inception, slumped in his chair. Here was an unqualified WASP, blessed with imposing demeanor, heading Washington's police force. Moab knew that he was smarter, harder working, and more highly skilled.

But it was the privileged class, the "old boys" network, what Moab called the "Establishment," that had kept him from reaching positions he deserved. The injustice of it all tormented him.

Moab's great-grandparents had emigrated from Russia to Palestine in the late 1920s, as part of a multi-national Jewish brigade that began irrigating deserts, sinking wells and planting forests in what they hoped would one day be their reclaimed homeland.

It was a hard life, and Moab's father, whose ambitions leaned more to the secular, abandoned Tel Aviv for the more cosmopolitan Beirut in the early 1960s. There he had married an expatriate Palestinian woman, making the detective half-Jewish and half-Muslim, although they raised him as neither; they knew the history of excessive bloodshed committed in the name of piety.

Their dream had always been to immigrate to the United States. Despite the fate of preceding waves of immigrants, who often lived cramped lives in tenements, working away in sweatshops, the myth of America's unfettered riches had an unwavering hold on their imagination.

When their son was born, they had called him Moab, because it was a name with important historical symbolism. The geographical area of Moab was located east of the Dead Sea, in present-day Jordan. In biblical times, the varying faiths of the inhabitants often caused conflict. Jeremiah's Old Testament prophecies had railed against the area and its people: "Their madmen will be silenced and the sword will follow, causing Moab's devastation." King David had finally brought peace to the country, and Moab's parents had hoped their son, in some small way, might help bring harmony between Muslims and Jews.

When Moab was about ten, his parents finally made the move to the U.S., but despite years of toil and hope, they were crushed by a grinding economic system that lavishly benefitted a lucky few, while leaving the rest to fend for themselves in an increasingly bleak landscape. They died disillusioned, never able to achieve any semblance of the American dream.

Moab watched his parents struggle helplessly, at the hands of forces beyond their control; as he saw it, life in these United States was too often a cruel and hollow joke. The ascendancy of a moron like the police superintendent was just one more example, he thought.

❖

The police superintendent forged ahead with his dogmatic lecture on Islamic terrorist groups. His subordinates were compelled to listen, but kept their opinions to themselves. Moab, however, as the leader of D.C.'s counterterrorism unit, had no such compunction.

"Kind of jumping to conclusions, aren't you, Superintendent?" he asked irritably.

Surprised by this display of impertinence, the superintendent banged his thermos down on the desk, spilling coffee on his immaculate blotter. "We aren't going to be dithering around. Most exceptional police work is based on instinct, and mine tells me to concentrate on the Muslim Brotherhood, Al Qaeda, and Hezbollah." Despite his bluster, the superintendent was relatively clueless about constantly changing political conditions.

Although the ongoing environmental degradation had

triggered alarming hotspots of regional anarchy, a certain precarious stability had been achieved in most of the so-called developed world, as major global players had decided that it was better to collude and divvy up what spoils remained, then fight one another other dwindling resources.

In the spirit of cynical cooperation, the Christian and Islamic worlds had called a truce of sorts. Both camps labored to quell the extremist elements within their midst, but achieving permanent peace remained elusive. New agitators periodically and inevitably rose to prominence.

"Good cops listen to their inner voice," the superintendent was saying. "You should try it some time, Detective." Sure, Moab thought to himself, the "inner voice." He'd often heard people like the superintendent speak of the voice of some higher power. Talk about fanaticism. Moab had concluded that there was just as much in Washington as Gaza or Riyadh.

The superintendent now turned his attention to listing groups with representation in D.C. that fostered Middle Eastern theocracy.

"First we have the Muslim Brotherhood," he said, writing the name on an easel tablet. "It is one of the oldest fundamentalist groups, started in Egypt in the 1920s. Early on it was the most powerful anti-colonial movement in the Middle East, responsible for the assassination of British citizens." The superintendent was showing an unexpected scholarly side, the detective had to admit. "The Brotherhood's main argument has been that the West corrupts the sanctity of the family by encouraging the independence of women. It has been a movement of angry men losing control."

The four women exchanged knowing glances; they knew the problem all too well.

"Second is Hezbollah, the military party founded during the Lebanese civil war in the early 1980s to fight Israel in southern Lebanon. During this period, Hezbollah also engineered the bombing of the American embassy and U.S. Marine headquarters in Beirut, killing more than three hundred people.

"Third is Al Qaeda, created in the late 1980s by Osama bin Laden, about the time the Russians withdrew from Afghanistan. He was, of course, the mastermind behind 9/11, the deadliest foreign attack on U.S. soil since Pearl Harbor. Though never captured and long deceased, bin Laden established bases around the world for recruiting operatives and disseminating jihad."

Moab had to acknowledge that the superintendent had articulated a fairly accurate historical, though hardly up-to-date summary of key Islamic sects.

"As I've said, the first thing I want done is to have Mr. Jaffee's landlady thoroughly interrogated, and his apartment building turned upside down and inside out. Then we'll talk to people at the local mosque."

# CHAPTER TWELVE

**As the police superintendent** had noted, Joshua Jaffee's landlady was Lebanese. She was a member of the Hassan family, which had been among the most dominant clans in Lebanon for centuries. After the end of World War I, when the Ottoman Empire collapsed and the West began controlling the Middle East, the Hassans, ever agile, ingratiated themselves with the British and French. They had witnessed the instability the West's imperial ambitions had caused by carving the region into arbitrary nation-states, heedlessly throwing Kurds, Sunnis, and Shiites together. The Hassan family was simply being practical, aligning itself with whoever held power.

As the 1920s began, the Hassan family had the money to join other members of the international privileged class celebrating the "decade of the endless party." In the Middle East's secular and religious mix, the Hassans sided with secularism. Their wealth dated to the age of Suleiman the Magnificent, the sixteenth century sultan of the Ottoman Empire. Early on they had accumulated huge tracts of land, and, as time went by, the family had further enlarged its fortune by capitalizing on the discovery of oil in the Middle East.

The family occupied a medieval fortified residence situated on the edge of a rocky precipice just south of Beirut. Malik

Hassan and his sister Malika were among the latest to have grown up within its walls, and, as part of a Westernized Lebanese elite, to have attended the American University in Beirut.

Though Malik was the oldest, he had obstinately refused to accept the role of many firstborns, to become a responsible, goal-driven example for his younger siblings. His education in Beirut had been followed by a brief stint at Oxford, but he had failed to graduate, failed to take a position in the family business, failed to join the exclusive Beirut club his great-grandfather had co-founded, and failed to live up to every other expectation his family had of him.

Acknowledging that their son might have, as his mother euphemistically put it, "lost his way a bit," his parents had him run a gauntlet of psychiatrists, tutors, hypnotists, and other guides and sages. Finally throwing up their hands in frustration, his parents set up a trust fund for him managed by Washington, D.C.'s largest bank, with whom the family dealt as part of their international network of affluence. They thought that the U.S. would be a safer place for someone like their son, giving him a chance to make a new start. In 2010, he had immigrated to Washington. He eagerly embraced the chance to move to the country of F. Scott Fitzgerald, that chronicler of American possibility.

Growing up, one of the few memories Malik had of his grandfather was listening to him read from his favorite book,

*The Great Gatsby.* The passage Malik had nearly committed to memory described a Gatsby summer party: "There were enough colored lights to make a Christmas tree of Gatsby's enormous garden. On buffet tables, spiced baked hams crowded against salads of harlequin designs and pastry pigs and turkey bewitched to a dark gold. By seven o'clock the orchestra arrived, with a whole pit full of oboes and trombones and saxophones and violas and cornets and piccolos and low and high drums. The halls and salons and verandas were gaudy with primary colors, beyond the dreams of Castile." This was Malik's vision of paradise—not a surfeit of beguiling female virgins—but the dreamy romance of an F. Scott Fitzgerald novel.

And America was also the home of Hollywood. The eternal escapist, Malik loved everything about the movies: the villains, the heroes, the big stars, the second bananas. He had spent most of his waking hours at Oxford watching videos of movie classics. Thus it was only natural that after he had settled in Washington, with plenty of money and nothing better to do, he bought the old Orpheum theatre. You could catch sight of him behind the popcorn concession, taking tickets, selling tickets, closing up at night, opening up during the day. He had become as defined by theatrical images, fantasies, and peeling paint as the theatre itself.

Malik's younger sister Malika soon joined her brother in D.C., seeking a more open lifestyle than she could find in Beirut, as fundamentalists began to reassert their dominance after decades of Westernization. Though she shed her veil, she hung on to her faith, remaining a devout though staunchly moderate Muslim.

Independent-minded since early childhood, Malika had purchased a small sixteen-unit apartment building after she arrived, occupying one of the apartments herself and managing the others. She had bought in a neighborhood that was a vibrant enclave of Arabic-language bookstores and kebab houses, where bearded men in long white robes continued to smoke water pipes in the tea shops, and black-veiled women pushed baby strollers into stores advertising halal meat. When you got off the subway station at Dupont Circle, it felt more like Kuwait City or Baghdad than the capital of the United States.

Thus it was that the morning after the police briefing, following the superintendent's instructions, Detective Moab found himself, with a fellow police officer at his side, pushing a buzzer at Joshua Jaffee's apartment building. A raucous, heavily accented voice ordered them in.

Although Malika's name meant "queen" in Arabic, the squat, dumpy little woman who met the detective and his comrade at the door had anything but a regal bearing. Moab began by inquiring if she was aware of the recent tragedy at the Lincoln Memorial.

"Do I look like I have the brains of a pack animal?" she barked.

It was a curious expression, delivered with such vehemence that the detective's associate took a few steps backwards, as if trying to shield himself from imminent attack. Moab narrowed his gaze, thinking unkindly, "Not the brains, but perhaps the looks." Forcing himself to be more tactful, he responded with a bland, "Well, of course not, ma'am."

Malika impatiently waved her hand, indicating a resentful willingness to continue. "I read all about it in the papers. What an interesting thing to happen. Mr. Jaffee, as you obviously know, was a tenant of mine."

The detective waited for signs of sympathy for the victim, even a perfunctory, "Oh, it's so tragic." With none forthcoming, he resumed his questioning.

"Tell me, ma'am, were you, or to your knowledge any of your neighbors, closely acquainted with the deceased?"

"He was not a social creature," she replied, "but I likely was as familiar with him as anyone here in the building."

Moab knew all about the Hassans. With roots in southern Lebanon, the family's close ties with Hezbollah had long been assumed, their Westernized ways notwithstanding. He decided to go on a fishing expedition, and, drawing his bushy eyebrows into an impressive frown, he growled, "Let's be honest, ma'am, you must have disliked Mr. Jaffee intensely. I can't imagine why you even rented to him, unless you had some ulterior motive. No one detests Jews more than Shiite members of Hezbollah, and no one has stronger connections to Hezbollah than your family."

Malika pursed her lips, in a supreme effort to control her temper. "By the way you reference Hezbollah, you suggest an organization I'm not familiar with. The Hezbollah I know helps run hospitals and schools in my home country."

"Now, Ms. Hassan," said Moab patronizingly, "I know for a fact that your father, a past member of the Lebanese parliament, once supported the theocratic Shiite Iranian Revolution, and the establishment of a Shiite government in Lebanon."

Malika refused to be baited. "If you have proof that I have committed a crime, then arrest me."

The detective shook his head in disgust. "All right, so what can you tell us about Jaffee? Hobbies? Social life? What?"

"You'll find a large stamp collection in his room, and despite his unappealing appearance and behavior, he had his female friends. The tall, thin, dark-haired one I saw the most. I think he told me she worked for an advertising agency. Then there was the shorter, heavier blonde—"

Moab cut her off brusquely, and asked to see Jaffee's room. His partner, trailing behind, whispered, "Hey, how come you stopped the interrogation? I think she has a lot more to tell."

"You think? You think? Trying to think only gets you in trouble."

Opening the door to Jaffee's room, they were greeted by what looked like the site of some catastrophic weather event. Malika seemed as surprised as anyone.

Dishes, books, towels, trash were strewn every which way. The place was sparsely decorated, with a single window looking out over an asphalt parking lot and an adjacent building. The floors had been covered by two cheap rugs. They were clearly in their declining years, faded and threadbare in spots. One of them had been tossed carelessly from its original location on the floor, visible by the dustless rectangle where it had lain, and had landed on top of a standing lamp.

As Moab entered, he saw the apartment was virtually a single living area, with a small kitchen tucked in one corner, partially hidden by a screen, and the door to a tiny bathroom in another corner; a bed and table occupied the center of the room. An expensively bound copy of the Torah lay conspicuously amongst the debris, and a large photograph rested on a pillow sitting dead-center on the bed.

It showed a young child standing hand in hand with a woman in her late twenties, wearing a vaguely military-looking uniform. Moab noticed that the photograph had no tears or rips; it was as if, in contrast to the disarray everywhere else, someone had carefully removed it from its frame, which was lying a few feet away, and had delicately placed it where it was sure to be seen.

The kitchen area contained an assortment of partially matching plates, cups, and silverware. The bathroom had its agglomeration of aftershave lotion, razor blades, and other male grooming paraphernalia. Rifling through the items that remained in the chest of drawers produced nothing notable; a sock was a sock was a sock. Moab guessed the wardrobe, on one side of the window, had probably contained a sports jacket, a half-dozen ties, a sweater or two, and a couple of coats; all these articles had also taken flight, and had landed in sundry locations around the room.

What stood out, almost enshrined in the only remaining open corner, was what Malika had mentioned, what appeared to be a rather remarkable stamp collection, sitting untouched in a glass-fronted bookcase. Besides the photograph, this was the only part of the apartment that had been treated respectfully. No one had laid a finger on the several stamp albums, with their patchwork of small, colored pieces of perforated paper precariously clinging to each page.

Having completed their inspection, Moab and his assistant left the room, preceded by Malika. The lower-ranking officer secured the door until the official crime lab team could make its search, and placed the obligatory rows of yellow tape across the entrance.

❖

Unbeknownst to anyone, Joshua Jaffe had been a post office mole, burrowing about not only within the main post office's storage areas, but also the archives of the old post office and the national postal museum. He had explored every nook and cranny of Washington's decrepit post office system, obsessively combing through stacks of shelves filled with ancient post office historical documents, bureaucratic housekeeping records, meeting minutes of long abandoned committees. No amount of minutia escaped his curiosity.

There were hundreds of books on the history of the post office and the history of stamp collecting. Jaffe had read most of them. The story of the Inverted Jenny was known to any serious stamp collector. One day in 1918, William T. Robey had stopped at his local post office and asked to purchase a sheet of airmail stamps. As the postal clerk had placed the one-hundred-stamp sheet in front of him, Robey had been hard pressed to maintain his composure.

The airplane pictured on each stamp was flying upside down. Mistakes were what collectors sought as the Holy Grail. Even for the U.S. post office, the printing of mistakes was unusual, and those that did occur rarely reached the public.

Robey was an avid collector in the Washington area, and he loved notoriety. Within hours the news of his discovery had spread rapidly, both within the stamp collecting community and at the post office.

Postal authorities immediately stopped the sale of the Inverted Jenny, informing the public that, except for Robey's one-hundred-stamp sheet, all copies had been destroyed. If the error had been limited to no more than a single proof, which meant at least three other panes had been printed, only Robey's flawed stamps would be in circulation.

The most affluent of the country's collectors sought out Bill Robey, and after days of negotiation, his Inverted Jennies were sold for fifteen thousand dollars, a rather princely sum at the time. Over the years, the full sheet was split into a variety of smaller segments, even into individual stamps.

Then, sitting on a stool one lazy afternoon, in an abandoned aisle of post office stacks, Jaffe experienced the same heart-stopping excitement William Robey had felt in 1918. As he opened an old, dusty folder, he discovered a *second* sheet of Inverted Jennies. His hands, his entire body began quivering. He felt nauseated, ecstatic. Somehow, this sheet had survived the attempted destruction of all such sheets on that celebrated day in 1918. Uncertain as to how to deal with his discovery, he had hidden the sheet of stamps, which measured about ten inches square, behind the sole photograph in his sparsely decorated apartment.

# CHAPTER THIRTEEN

**At his next** investigative meeting, the superintendent paced nervously about his office, crisscrossing in front of his dozen subordinates seated in the area facing his desk. They sometimes found themselves staring at empty space, when in his agitation the superintendent walked in a circle around the room.

Detective Moab reported on his visit to Jaffee's apartment, describing its disheveled condition and the discovery of the stamp collection. He discussed Malika Hassan's reference to Jaffee's occasional dark-haired female companion. "Ms. Hassan denied being any kind of Islamic zealot," he continued, "but I know that she is a prominent presence at her local mosque."

"What do you mean by that?" the superintendent rasped. He moved towards the detective with thermos raised, as if to strike him, only to pause, unscrew the cap and pour some coffee into a cup on his desk.

"You want me to find the definition of 'prominent' for you in the dictionary?" Moab asked, their mutual hostility now in full flower. The superintendent instructed Moab to follow up on the "philatelic" lead, hoping to fluster the detective with the use of the somewhat esoteric word. Moab knew its meaning, and just nodded calmly.

❖

That afternoon, Traveler, at the superintendent's behest, made a reconnaissance visit to the mosque near Malika's apartment. The mosque consisted of a prayer hall and a walled courtyard where worshippers often congregated. Minarets stood at the corner of each wall. As Traveler entered the holy place, he removed his shoes and washed his hands at one of the fountains outside the prayer room.

Followers of Islam are required by their faith to pray five times a day facing the holy city of Mecca. Traveler watched the proceedings as the assembled faithful went through their ritual bowing, kneeling and prostration. He listened to a recitation from the first chapter of the Quran. When the imam finished, the worshippers looked first over their right shoulders, then their left, saying each time, "Peace be on you and the mercy of Allah."

Recognizing Traveler as a stranger to the mosque, the imam approached and greeted him. "Welcome to our house of worship," he said.

The two men moved to a quiet, shaded corner. "It's not very luxurious here, certainly by Western religious standards, but Muslims are a simple people," the imam said. As they settled onto concrete benches, the imam asked, "Are you at all familiar with our holy book?"

"Somewhat," Traveler replied. "You see, I'm a journalist by trade, and as part of my work I've had occasion to study your religion."

Guessing that Traveler's knowledge of Islam was more political than religious, the imam continued, "I would suspect that in your career you may have focused on such organizations as Hezbollah and the Muslim Brotherhood. These groups have never represented mainstream Islam. Ours is not, as many have characterized it, a violent religion. It is only a few renegades who have badly misrepresented us."

Traveler suspected this was true. The destruction of the Twin Towers at the turn of the century—which had allowed the American president the pretext to declare "war" against a small band of discontented militants—was a decision prompted by incompetence and hubris, that had cost the nation dearly.

Traveler now addressed the specific reason for his visit. "I've been asked to help in the investigation of the recent Lincoln Memorial bombing. The victim's landlady, Malika Hassan, is, I believe, one of your members."

"Oh, yes. Both she and her brother worship here. She attends more regularly. Malik, I fear, has almost completely embraced Western material culture. His commitment to Islam is frail at best, but he is a kind, inoffensive man."

"If my information is correct, Mr. Jaffee once picketed this mosque, did he not?" asked Traveler.

"That is correct. He felt strongly that Palestine was a land that belonged exclusively to the Jews, and he exercised his freedom of speech to express that view. This is one of the wonderful rights granted by the Constitution that we Islamic-Americans honor always." He rose from his seat, and said, "I'm afraid I've shared with you what little I know," indicating the conversation was over.

"Thank you for your time, imam."

"You are welcome. Allah be with you."

# CHAPTER FOURTEEN

**In English-speaking circles,** Sophia Azarmedukht was usually known as Sophia A., or simply Sophia. She took no offense, knowing many found her name unpronounceable. In any case, she was extremely proud of her heritage as, according to family history, she was descended from seventh century Persian royalty.

In advertising circles, she was regarded as brilliant. A creative consultant for one of the top U.S. advertising agencies, she was widely given credit for some of America's most famous advertising campaigns.

It didn't hurt her professional reputation that men were immediately drawn to her physically. She was a stunning five feet, ten inches, with radiant olive skin and an incandescent smile. In her late thirties, she projected genuine erotic energy, but seemed unaware of, and unaffected by it.

The Chairman, of course, knew about her, as he knew about anyone who possessed unique skills that might possibly be exploited. He had, in fact, brought her into his network several months before Traveler's and Savant's visit to the Chairman's compound, when he had asked her to visit with a trusted subordinate for dinner at the historic Washington Hotel.

That evening the hotel restaurant was filled with the usual suspects: several of the city's better known politicians, political operatives, corporate chiefs, and lobbyists. The restaurant always kept the lighting subdued, perhaps to soften the facial imperfections of many of its aging diners, or to provide an obscured atmosphere for the brewing of conspiratorial plots.

"Lovely to meet you," Sophia said as she introduced herself to the subordinate, one of the Chairman's legions of indistinguishable good-looking men in expensive forgettable suits.

After they had ordered, the subordinate wasted little time. "The Chairman has a very serious business proposal to make, Sophia, that I think you will find intriguing.

"He believes that we have reached a political breaking point in this country. We have come close before, but the Chairman thinks that voters are finally ready to elect a third party, and that neither the Republicans nor the Democrats have the will or resources to successfully defend themselves."

Sophia knew that if anyone was capable of masterminding such a changing of the guard, it was the Chairman.

"I don't mean to be rude," she said, "but why are you discussing this with me?" Her voice was unusually melodic, softening and strengthening, her manner gracious yet detached.

As she waited for an answer, their meals arrived, and she began slicing into her rare steak. After they had both spent some minutes eating, Sophia's dinner partner put his fork down, and gave her a brief introduction to the New Politics concept.

That task completed, he explained that the Chairman "hoped" (a euphemism being attributed to a man whose offers were seldom refused) that Sophia would agree to promote the New Politics and its agenda—to spearhead the advertising and communications efforts to raise visibility for the New Politics. "In other words," the subordinate said, "the Chairman will purchase the banners to be waved, and you will create the messages to be written on them."

"So, can you tell me more specifically what the Chairman envisions as the basic message for the New Politics?" Sophia asked, technically neither accepting nor rejecting the "offer"— but she was clearly intrigued.

The subordinate ignored the question. "He knows that advertising usually requires the message be captured in twenty-five words or less, but this one may be a little more complicated. Still, one of your tasks will be to render it in bumper-sticker format for easier voter consumption."

The man resumed eating, dividing his food into parcels on his plate, using his fork to separate the protein from the starches and the greens, arranging them like small dwellings within the outer wall of the plate's border.

"The Chairman is certain," he now continued, "that the electorate ultimately votes on the basis of a candidate's perceived strength. Issues become so complex and circumstances change so quickly that voters choose to embrace a candidate depending on whether or not they feel he is a strong leader, that he can 'get things done.'"

That pronouncement apparently ended the business portion of their meeting. They finished their entrees trading light gossip and small talk about current Washington entertainment fare. After dessert, the subordinate held up his scotch on the rocks, swirled the liquid so the ice cubes clinked quietly, and said, "To victory. The Chairman wants to discuss this matter with you personally, and would like to see you within the week. He will have the appropriate arrangements made."

❖

Within days, Sophia was whisked by private jet and helicopter to the Chairman's compound. She settled in at the island's guest lodgings in the morning; after lunch, she was transported to the Chairman's central command complex.

Sophia followed a ritual for entering the compound similar to the one Traveler would later experience; before long, she found herself seated in the Chairman's dark office.

Even in the shadows, the Chairman could appreciate Sophia's extraordinary attractiveness, though he kept his thoughts to himself. "Thank you for coming," was all he said.

"It's my pleasure," Sophia replied.

The Chairman spent the first part of the meeting on the same preliminaries that would later define his session with

Traveler: explaining the Alfred E. Neuman mask, the darkened conditions, the blood and urine specimens. Finally, he broached the major item on his agenda; in contrast to many of his meetings, he went straight to the point.

"Sophia, as my subordinate has explained, I need you to help me launch a New Politics party. As the project progresses, I'll fill you in on the details. At this point, let me simply say that the party will be built around the theme of bringing forceful, independent decision-making back to politics. Not an original claim, to be sure, which means that we must substantiate it with unusually captivating evidence.

"Strength and independence imply two things, honesty and competence. But honesty is of lesser significance. People vote for someone not simply because they believe he is telling the truth, but because they think he is competent enough and strong enough to carry out what he says he will do. Are you with me, Sophia?"

"I am indeed," she replied. The New Politics articulated in sinister darkness.

"Good. Now, the challenging part will be to persuade voters that the two men I will select as leaders of the party are not only worthy of their support, but irresistibly so. How this is accomplished will be up to you and me.

"I am not at liberty to reveal their names to you at this moment, but I believe the electorate will accept them as the kind of charismatic revolutionaries the times we live in demand.

Their careers have demonstrated achievement in numerous areas. People perceive them as bright and bold. What voters must be shown—and I know this may sound contradictory—is both a magnification as well as an obfuscation of those qualities. That is where the real passes into illusion. It's the work of the magician, requiring the application of your extraordinary creative gifts."

Sophia knew about reality and illusion. She had moved to England at a very early age, when her family left Iran several years after the Shah had been deposed in 1979. Her first husband had been a member of the House of Lords. Young and inexperienced, she had initially been bewitched by the man's fame and surface charm. Behind this public facade was a philandering alcoholic. It was an elaborate masquerade that ended prematurely in a drunken automobile accident, leaving Sophia a widow at age twenty-two.

The Chairman ended their discussion, promising that more would be revealed in good time. Leaving the island, Sophia found herself with exhilarating anticipation battling ominous uncertainty.

# CHAPTER FIFTEEN

**Someone highly placed** had directed that Traveler meet with Malik Hassan, who had identified Joshua Jaffee as a regular customer at his theatre when police had canvassed the neighborhood a few days earlier. Malik had also mentioned, as had his sister, a "dark-haired woman" who had occasionally accompanied the victim to the movies. Now Traveler was to interview him more extensively within the friendly confines of Hassan's beloved theatre. The appointment had already been made, and Malik was expecting him.

The D.C. police superintendent had also been instructed to have Traveler draw on Savant's artistic expertise; skill as a sketch artist was among his multiple talents.

Upon their arrival at the Orpheum, Traveler introduced himself and Savant to Malik. He explained that they would be sketching a portrait of the "dark-haired woman" whom Malik had indicated he'd seen with Jaffee at the theatre.

Malik had an unmistakable fey quality. Traveler had never felt comfortable around effeminate men, a legacy of his Southern Christian upbringing, but he worked hard to maintain a professional demeanor. He started by going over well-trod ground. "I understand that you have identified Mr. Jaffee as a known patron of the Orpheum."

"That is correct."

"I further understand that you had often observed him with a tall, dark-haired lady," Traveler said. "Now, my associate here, who is an accomplished artist, will begin drawing the features of a woman's face, in rough form. We'd appreciate it if you'd add comments and corrections as he goes along. Hopefully the end result will be a likeness of the woman you saw accompanying Jaffee."

Savant's initial pencil strokes created an oval, generic facial outline. Malik enthusiastically entered into the exercise, at the same time lurching into a monologue, largely about the movies.

"I love the Jazz Age," he began, then jumped to, "Now *Two Women*, there was a picture. It made Sophia Loren famous, of course, winning her the Oscar for best actress in 1960."

Savant couldn't help himself. "You had to love her earlier films, too, like *Boy on a Dolphin*, and her perfect casting with Anthony Perkins in *Desire Under the Elms*."

Malik, pleasantly surprised by Savant's cinematic erudition, replied, "Yes, indeed, and then she co-starred in two films with Cary Grant, *The Pride and the Passion*, and later in that romantic comedy, *Houseboat*. Cary Grant was also in the Alfred Hitchcock movie, of course, where he's chased by a crop-duster."

Malik paused to instruct Savant on the shape of the woman's mouth. "The lips are fuller, with a pouting, sensual appearance."

He returned to his musings about the cinema. "*North by Northwest* was one of Jaffee's favorite movies, especially the scene where the plane barnstorms after Cary Grant, flying upside down, every which way. He watched the movie dozens of times, and we talked about the airplane scene at length.

"He'd exclaim, 'Look at it! A biplane flying upside down. What freedom! What freedom!' "

Malik continued his impromptu lecture on movie history, interspersed with directions for Savant, and the sketch began to take shape. Then, apparently tiring of the silver screen, Malik turned to the printed page.

"Ah, yes, the Jazz Age," he sighed. "There has never been a better writer than Fitzgerald. I identify with his protagonists… 'I have lost myself. I cannot tell you the hour when, or the day of the week, the month or the year,' " he continued, paraphrasing a simpering character from *Tender Is the Night*. " 'There has always been some element of loneliness involved. No one will attend my funeral. No one will be interested. Interested, I mean, with that intense personal interest to which everyone has some vague right at the end.' "

Savant eagerly added his perspective. "You know, I think that's exactly the way Fitzgerald himself felt at the end of his life. So sad." But Malik was already leaving that subject behind, shifting gears again. "Yeah, I'd put Sophia Loren up against any of them. Audrey Hepburn, Betty Grable, Jodie Foster, Maureen O'Sullivan, even the great Garbo. Sophia Loren was something special." Fifteen more minutes passed with his disjointed observations about a bygone era before Savant completed the portrait to Malik's satisfaction.

"She looks a lot like Sophia Loren, doesn't she?" Savant said.

"Indeed," Malik beamed.

❖

Though he believed he was likely on the proverbial wild goose chase, Traveler found himself later that afternoon en route to Malika Hassan's apartment. He rang the doorbell and heard her shrill voice uttering unintelligible words; as he waited, he drew his considerable frame up to its full height, as if girding himself for the small but powerful force on the other side of the door.

She opened it with a glare. After introducing himself, Traveler said, "I know that several police officers have already been here to speak with you, have interviewed your tenants, and that the police lab crew has gone through Mr. Jaffee's premises. But I'm here to see if you might recognize a possible suspect from an artist's sketch." Traveler handed her the sketch developed that morning without identifying its origin.

She studied it carefully for several moments. "If I'm not mistaken, this looks very much like one of Jaffee's lady friends."

Traveler was startled. He'd been certain that her brother had simply wasted their time with his Sophia Loren nonsense. "You're sure?"

"Absolutely. I always thought she was unexpectedly attractive, considering Jaffee's looks and all."

"Might you know anything more about her?"

"As I explained to the officers, I only saw her come and go a couple of times. I think I heard Jaffee say once that she worked in advertising."

"Would you mind if I came in?"

"I suppose not," Malika replied hesitantly.

Her apartment was decorated with mementos of a prosperous upbringing. "There seems to be quite a record of the past here," Traveler said.

"Well, yes, I guess so. The Hassans have been one of the most prominent families in the Middle East for hundreds of years. May I offer you a beverage?"

"I would welcome a cup of coffee with sugar, if you have it." Malika left the room, returning with an ornately patterned bone china cup and saucer.

"One benefit, if you can call it that," she then said, "is after you've been raised in Lebanon, life can no longer deal you many surprises. That is why the killing of my tenant didn't shock me. It has been more peaceful of late, but Lebanon has a history where the prospect of dying a random death has been a constant."

Malika seemed to suddenly be somewhere else, mentally plumbing unknown depths. Traveler sensed their brief conversation had come to an end. "I will leave you now," he said, and astonished himself by adding as he left, "Allah be with you."

# CHAPTER SIXTEEN

**The day was overcast**, and Detective Moab was inching his way through the snarl of D.C. traffic. He was on his way to St. John's Parish House, where the Washington Philatelic Society met, to see the society's director.

St. John's Parish House was one of Washington's prime historical sites, and its interior, though not spacious, exuded a certain aura of self-assurance; it was as if the walls were smugly thinking, "We have already survived for several human lifetimes."

As soon as he entered, Moab picked up a leaflet from a pile on a small table at the front of the narthex. It appeared to be a pamphlet published by the Philatelic Society with a list of club functions for the year. Glancing at it, he observed how obscure and even comical stamp collecting could be. He noted that he had already missed the meetings featuring "The Postal History of the Czech Siberian Legion," as well as the "Masters of the Night" presentation, described as "an international award-winning thematic exhibit on the subject of bats."

The director appeared at the doorway of his office, off the main corridor, and ushered Moab in, motioning him to take a seat in one of the stiff high-backed wooden chairs lined up like soldiers in front of the director's desk.

The director seated himself behind the desk, a fussy, eighteenth century antique. "I gather that you are pursuing a case involving stamps in some important way. I've had a chance to review the collection the authorities sent over yesterday, and I must say that it does have its idiosyncrasies."

*Idiosyncrasies*, Moab thought, scowling. The director had the aristocratic affectations, the air of so-called "fine breeding" so typical of the Establishment types Moab detested. "Do you know much about stamps, Detective?" the director asked; to Moab, the question was dripping with condescension.

Annoyed, he emphatically responded, "Of course."

This was sufficient to launch the director on what would prove to be a major discourse. "Let me give you a little background. The first letters were those carried to and from members of English royalty. A network developed between a few towns, like London and Plymouth. The first postmark—not a stamp, mind you—was used in 1661."

Moab shifted his weight in a futile attempt to make himself comfortable in his hard, unyielding seat. *Pompous ass*, he thought.

"The British were the pioneers in issuing stamps to prepay postage on letters. An actual competition was organized to solicit stamp designs. Amazingly, more than two thousand entries were received. The famous 'penny black' stamps were first issued in 1840, shortly followed by the two pence blues. By the 1860s almost all countries had adopted stamps as a way of paying postage.

"In 1862, the U.S. Congress passed a stamp act to raise money to help fund the North's participation in the Civil War. Stamp laws were subsequently passed to fund the Spanish-American War and World War I."

Just as a way to interject his presence, Moab contemplated asking him about World War II, but before he could utter a word, the director surged onward.

"During World War II, the U.S. offered stamps to assist in financing that effort as well.

"Let us turn now to the topic of stamp collecting itself, one of the most popular hobbies in the world," he said, apparently finished with his introductory remarks and moving on to the main presentation. "Every kind of person, in every conceivable occupation and set of circumstances collects stamps. There is no country, despite continuing geographical boundary changes, where someone doesn't have a passion for stamp collecting.

"To editorialize for a moment, many collectors, myself among them, have mixed feelings about the ebb and flow of international politics. On the one hand, civil wars, wars between nation-states, police actions, terrorist activities, whatever, create opportunities for new stamps to be printed. That's good. On the other hand, these same kinds of events are disruptive for stamp collectors.

"We are people who tend to like order, and if you're an avid collector of African stamps, for example, you can hardly contain your frustration at the possibility that any one of those countries, at any time, might merge, cease to exist, conquer someone, or be conquered. Politics and warfare are continuing irritants."

Moab could hardly believe what he was hearing. The director was telling him that the strongest feelings he could muster against some of the greatest scourges of mankind were a sense of *irritation and inconvenience*. It just reaffirmed his conviction that these kinds of people lived in bubbles of arrogant, callous entitlement.

"In any case," the director continued, "stamp collecting is an activity with so many variables to it. Different types of paper, watermarks, inks, printing processes, perforation conditions, dates of cancellations. Then the varying types, the first-day covers, the commemoratives, the plate blocks—"

As the director finally paused for breath, Moab seized his chance to redirect the conversation towards Joshua Jaffee's collection. "Yes, but what was your assessment of the Lincoln Memorial case stamps?"

"Of course. Well, Mr. Jaffee clearly had a commitment to the hobby. His collection, mostly U.S. stamps, is quite comprehensive. The quality is good, though it lapses in places.

"In fact, and this is a curiosity, the unevenness of the collection makes it almost seem..." and here the director paused thoughtfully, before concluding with emphasis "...as if more than one person had assembled the stamps."

"I don't follow you," Moab said.

"Parts of the collection were obviously arranged with great care. In other sections, the work seems to have been done with less discrimination. Hinges are carelessly attached, entries in the album are off-kilter, that sort of thing."

"I'll include those observations in my report," Moab said dryly. "I'm sure they will prove valuable."

The director was oblivious to his mocking tone. "Then there's the aspect of theme collecting, where collectors concentrate on areas of special interest. In fact, the themes are almost unlimited—"

Fearing that the director was preparing another encyclopedic review, Moab quickly interjected, "Yes, I'm sure they are unlimited, but did you find any thematic patterns to Jaffee's collection?"

"Only one, perhaps—U.S. airmail stamps. Historically speaking, as you may know, America's most famous airmail stamp is called the Inverted Jenny. In 1918, it was mistakenly printed with a biplane flying upside down, and—"

Moab intervened once more. "I'm sure the history is fascinating," he said, "but I really must get back to the station."

"Sorry, old sport, but I do get carried away. Oh, I have taken the liberty of e-mailing to a Mr. Traveler, at his request, the names and phone numbers of the members of the stamp clubs that meet regularly in Washington." Moab thanked the director for his time, and prepared to take his leave.

Even though their encounters had been few and brief, he had come to dislike Traveler as another typical Establishment type. The journalist always seemed to be meddling, sticking his classically handsome nose in places where it didn't belong. He would be trouble. Moab just knew it.

❖

During his lengthy discussion with Moab, the director had not said anything about an unusual telephone call he had received shortly after the Lincoln Memorial bombing. The connection seemed flimsy, merely coincidental, but it was a puzzling confluence of events nonetheless.

The call had come from a stunning woman the director had met once or twice at Philatelic Society meetings. After introducing herself over the phone, she began, "I hope you may be able to help me with a small matter."

"Yes, of course," he replied eagerly, recalling her comeliness.

"I'm involved with creative development for one of the city's major advertising agencies, and we've been assigned a new client, an airline. I'm doing background work for a media campaign the agency is contemplating. The market research suggests that the public sees our client as cold and uncaring. Not an unusual perception these days, of course."

In fact, few airlines still existed. Fuel costs had skyrocketed, and people could no longer afford to travel much, only on the most special of occasions.

"We're considering a campaign to counter these perceptions…" her voice trailed off. "I apologize if I'm boring you with this."

"Not at all, not at all, my dear."

"Well, we're trying to create a warmer, more light-hearted 'personality,' you might call it, for our client. The TV campaign may include a series of vignettes where the CEO begins by referencing his airline's tradition of excellence. Then he weaves a story around an episode important in aviation history.

"To kick off the new campaign, we've tentatively selected an event with which I know you're familiar, the start of mail transportation by air, and the printing of the Inverted Jenny airmail stamp. We might have the CEO actually show a copy of the stamp, and make some clever quips about how his airline will do just about anything the customer asks, except fly the plane upside down; we haven't determined the exact dialogue yet, but I think you get the general idea."

"Yes, I do, but I'm afraid I'm still unclear as to how I might be of assistance."

"We're evaluating having the CEO make his points while in conversation with a noteworthy guest. As an example, for the ad featuring the Inverted Jenny, a possible guest might be a famous stamp collector.

"Which brings me to my specific request. Would you be able to provide the names of collectors who could afford to own, or, better yet, actually do own an Inverted Jenny? Using such a person would enhance our ad's credibility."

The director hesitated. "As you might imagine, given your own interest in stamps, this kind of collector guards his anonymity."

"I do understand that, but I also know that famous people, or wealthy people who want to be famous, occasionally spark to this kind of idea."

"Let me make some inquiries," the director finally said.

"I'm very grateful. I'll call again in a week or so."

❖

Traveler was growing bleary-eyed. He had been staring at the listings of the Washington, D.C. stamp clubs on his computer screen for the last several hours. Though weary, he felt compelled to examine each one in detail. After all, the attorney general was calling for updates almost daily.

It was amazing the number of stamp clubs that existed within the city and its immediate environs, Traveler thought. There appeared to be four major groups near the Capitol; the remainder the Philatelic Society director had catalogued alphabetically by city or town, starting with Aberdeen, Maryland.

All told, Traveler guessed that residing within his computer were membership lists for about thirty different organizations.

Taking the average number of members per club, and multiplying that by thirty came to...Traveler was too tired to complete the simple math.

What made people so fascinated by those silly little pieces of colored paper? And why couldn't there be fewer of them, both the pieces of paper and the people?

Traveler knew that the FBI's computer whiz kids could slice and dice these lists in a hundred different ways. He was working against heavy odds, with little chance of success, but he felt the need to do something, anything, to move the investigation along.

He had made an initial scan of the clubs' membership lists, without locating the name Joshua Jaffee, but hoped the murder victim might occasionally have attended club meetings, and in this way perhaps become acquainted with the dark-haired lady in question. Malika had remembered her as working "in advertising," so Traveler was cross-referencing and Googling names on the membership lists to determine each person's profession. He was humming *Luck Be a Lady Tonight*, when there on the screen was listed "advertising consultant." As a religious man, Traveler almost embraced it as a near-epiphany.

Early the next morning, Traveler pressed the phone numbers he had copied down the night before.

"Creative group. May I help you?" a perky voice said at the other end of the line.

"Yes, good morning. I represent the Washington, D.C. police department—"

"Oh heavens, I hope this isn't about those awful parking tickets. I promise—"

"No, no. I just need to speak with a Ms. Sophia...ah, I'm sorry but I'm afraid I can't pronounce her last name. It's about a matter under police investigation."

"Oh, thank goodness. Not about speaking with Ms. Sophia, you understand, but about—"

"Of course," Traveler replied. "Is she generally referred to as Ms. Sophia?"

"Yes. She understands the near impossibility, among English-speaking people, of pronouncing her last name."

"Is she available by any chance?"

"No, sir, I'm sorry, but she's away in Europe. She often sets her own schedule, and constantly flies back and forth between the U.S. and Europe or the Middle East."

"Yes, I understand. Would you describe more specifically her activities for the agency?"

"Before becoming a consultant, she was our most senior creative person, so the agency frequently asks her to work on advertising campaigns for our more important international clients. She's so busy it makes our heads spin. We often can't even keep track of her."

"I would imagine so, but can you tell me when she's expected back in Washington?"

"Actually, last night she left a message that she hoped to be in our office tomorrow, but her calendar here is always booked solid when she returns."

"I can appreciate that, but I absolutely must speak with her. Could you possibly pencil me in for thirty minutes? I promise you, that's all the time it will take."

"Let me see. I'm looking at what I suspect will be her schedule. Our agency chairman insists on seeing her first thing for an extensive update, so I'm afraid eight to noon is out. Followed by a major creative strategy meeting, that will likely consume the remainder of her day—"

"I'm sorry, but this is a matter of the greatest urgency," Traveler broke in impatiently. "Now, I don't want to cause an awkward situation here, like speaking to your chairman." Then, softening his tone, "I'm sure you want to do what's in Ms. Sophia's best interests."

"I'll tell the chairman a family emergency has come up and that the morning update will need to end by ten a.m. Then I'll make reservations for the two of you at a small restaurant I know she likes. Is that satisfactory?"

"Thank you. Let me give you my direct line."

❖

The Mediterranean Bar and Grill was not the kind of place where sophisticated, image-conscious types were likely to congregate. It was a workingman's pub in an ethnic neighborhood, and Traveler wondered what kind of big-shot consultant would choose it.

As he sat at a small table in the back corner of the room, he checked his watch. Only a couple of customers occupied the place, and they were sitting on bar stools at the counter. The meeting had been set for eleven a.m. It was already ten past.

Then she walked in.

She was stunning in an iridescent green pants suit, her hair perhaps a bit longer than Sophia Loren's, and dark strands occasionally fell across her eyes, veiling her face in a particularly fetching manner.

As she blinked, her lush eyelashes momentarily covered eyes of a smoldering charcoal hue. Traveler sensed almost viscerally the erotic yet unpretentious aura that seemed to surround her like an invisible halo.

Traveler's gaze remained riveted on her as she approached him. She was the only woman in the room, so she'd easily draw any man's attention; he knew, however, that even if he were passing her on a busy street, she would have been the instant object of his regard. As she walked to the back of the room, Traveler rose, awkwardly trying to hide his cane underneath the jacket he had hung over the back of his chair.

"You must be Mr. Traveler. I am Sophia Azarmedukht. For obvious reasons, most people simply call me Sophia," she said, offering him a firm handshake. Anticipating his curiosity, she continued, "If you're wondering why I chose this place, here are members of my Middle Eastern tribe, if you will," she said with a smile.

Neither knew the other had been drawn into the Chairman's New Politics scheme. This was the Chairman's typical modus operandi. He sometimes even assigned identical tasks to several individuals, to get different perspectives. Ultimately, hundreds would be employed to assure optimum execution of the New Politics vision. Most would not know more than a handful of their colleagues.

"Ms. Sophia," Traveler began, "thank you for meeting with me on such short notice. I understand that your consulting expertise is in high demand, so I won't take any more of your time than necessary. I simply need to ask you a few questions about someone who may have been an acquaintance."

"And who might this person be?" she asked, casually brushing the hair from her face; Traveler found this charming and provocative.

"Joshua Jaffee, the victim of the Lincoln Memorial bombing," he said.

Sophia gave him the semblance of a perplexed look. As he began describing the event and the victim, she immediately interrupted with, "Oh, dear! I didn't realize—I'm out of the country so much, and so preoccupied with business, seldom even following the news—" she stammered, impulsively reaching across the table to lightly touch Traveler's arm.

Keenly aware of her hand on his arm, Traveler nonetheless continued as nonchalantly as he could. "I understand, of course. We're trying to uncover clues about the identity of the assailants. You are certainly not a suspect, but you have been identified as knowing Mr. Jaffee."

"I can't believe it," she said softly, with the appearance of Jaffee's death beginning to sink in. "Joshua was a kind and gentle man."

"Can you tell me how the two of you met, and the nature of your relationship?" Traveler asked, then immediately regretted the blunt phrasing. "I'm sorry, I don't mean to pry into your personal life, but I must ask that you try to recall aspects of your relationship that could possibly relate to the case."

"I want to do anything I can to help. I considered him a friend," she said with seeming sincerity.

Although they had not yet ordered lunch, Sophia continued, "The only problem is that I need to return to the agency. My first few days back from an assignment are always frantic. Might we meet again later this afternoon?"

Nodding, Traveler asked, "Drinks, or an early dinner, perhaps?"

"I know this is an unusual request," she said, "but could you meet me at five at the Air and Space Museum? Joshua and I spent a good deal of time there. I'm optimistic it may jog my memory and bring back something important to the investigation. Afterwards, I'm afraid I'll need to return to the agency for a late session."

❖

At precisely five p.m., Sophia appeared in the museum lobby, looking radiant.

Traveler's thoughts turned unbidden to the Sermon on the Mount, where Jesus said that thoughts were as important as actions—specifically that a man who looked at a woman "with lust in his heart" was committing as grievous a sin as carnal knowledge. He tried to persuade himself that Jesus meant this to apply only to those who were married, but suspected he was attempting to get off on a technicality.

They walked together into the large exhibit hall. Traveler made a special effort to stride vigorously, despite the encumbrance of his cane. Sophia seemed to move synchronously with the rhythms of the universe.

"Joshua and I had a common interest in collecting airmail stamps," she said. "I think it was practically in my DNA. My father had been a dedicated stamp collector, and, in his final years in America, became obsessed with U.S. airmails. The two of us shared an unusually close bond. His obsessions often became mine. In any case, Joshua and I sometimes attended the philatelic club meetings held in the James Madison building, not too far from here. I can't recall our first conversation precisely. Maybe we met at the coffee machine, or accidently bumped into one another, and I made some innocuous remark. I'm sure he didn't initiate anything."

"Why do you say that?"

"I don't know how much you've learned," she paused, "but he was uncomfortable around women." Especially beautiful women, Traveler thought parenthetically.

"How well did you get to know him?" he inquired.

Sophia brushed aside her hair again, a gesture mesmerizing to Traveler.

"Not well. He was very private, and told me he rarely spent time with others."

"And the obvious differences in your ethnic backgrounds weren't a problem?"

"Not really. I'm perhaps more secular than religious. My parents came from Iran, and we Persians tend to be worldlier."

By now the two had stopped at the "Women Pilots in America" display, which featured Amelia Earhart and the plane she piloted in her nonstop flight across the Atlantic in 1932.

As Sophia turned towards Traveler, she tilted her head slightly upwards to look directly into his eyes, and lowered her voice to a husky whisper. "He enjoyed this part of the museum the most. His aunt, who I gathered raised him, had been a stewardess. From what the poor man said, you felt that without her he might have been even more lost than he already was."

Traveler paused, and said, "I must ask you an indiscreet question."

"Oh," Sophia mirthfully replied, "I've been asked more indiscreet questions than the Quran has interpretations."

Traveler laughed in return. "We're having difficulty finding out much about Mr. Jaffee's background, so what was there about him that you found intriguing, especially when he apparently repelled most others?"

The question seemed to bemuse her. "Why, Mr. Traveler, a man as cosmopolitan as you must know that when it comes to such matters between a man and a woman, there is often a certain *je ne sais quoi*."

"Well, yes, I suppose so," faltered Traveler, now eager to drop the subject. "We didn't find much in his apartment. Did you ever notice anything there that might be of help to this case?"

"He had so few personal possessions. I only remember the photograph of him as a small boy, holding his aunt's hand, and the stamp collection, of course."

"Please try and remember carefully. Was there ever anything else he talked about or that you saw which might be significant?"

"Let me see. He was so practiced at not letting you get too close. But, yes—I don't know why I didn't recall it before—he once talked about collecting things in general. As a kid, he said, he had an insect collection that was his pride and joy."

Sophia grew pensive. "In my life, I have seen some of the terrible things that humans can do to one another. He always seemed so harmless, though. Yet I do remember there was this one occasion when he made me genuinely queasy.

"Again, I'm surprised that I had forgotten the incident, because his exact words were so poignant. He was describing his insect collection as his 'little catatonic victims of formaldehyde.' The casual cruelty of it was so unlike him. He said, 'I wanted to make them feel the way I felt. When I stuck the pins through their abdomens, I liked to hear the shells crunch.' "

Now that her powers of recollection had stirred, another memory rose to consciousness. "And then there was a time that seemed to unusually disturb him. It was one of those peculiar little incidents that you ordinarily might not recall—"

Traveler seized her hand, scarcely realizing he was touching her. "Yes? Go on."

"It happened after a movie, I think, and we had gone back to his apartment for tea, as we sometimes did. He was wearing his only sports jacket. He must have bought it years before, and I recognized it as extremely expensive—by one of those high-end designers—Canali, Versace? Maybe Burberry? In any case, it had become a bit ragged, and it had all those inside pockets that he'd fill with notes and other miscellany. I'm not sure what he was looking for, but as he pulled his hand from one of the pockets, a matchbook fell to the floor.

"Since it fell closest to me, I picked it up. You could hardly read the writing on it because it was so faded and worn, but I made out 'Flamingo, NYC.' Then, before I had time to observe it more closely, he so rudely snatched it out of my hand that otherwise I don't think I would have given it another thought."

# CHAPTER SEVENTEEN

**Reverend Christian** was in the doldrums. Congregation membership had been in persistent decline. Donations were down, and his prominence had peaked years ago. His cable TV show still drew a loyal audience, but it was hardly the millions of subscribers he'd once had. And his political outreach program had only a smattering of zealous local chapters. The Reverend Christian ached to return to the glory years.

Critics had long vilified him as hypocrisy incarnate. He was alleged to have once asserted, "Christianity, you know, is actually just a big lie." Religious fundamentalism was like any other business, of course. Revenues needed to exceed costs. Market share must be defended.

"Gentlemen," the Reverend began, at the conclusion of the morning's staff review of the latest market research, "we've got to do something to turn this around. We need a hot button to push. Any suggestions?" His associates had heard him ask this question dozens of times.

One difference this morning, however, was the presence of Sophia Azarmedukht. Subsequent to her initial meeting with the Chairman, he had identified his president and vice president candidates for the 2024 election. The Chairman had also revealed his stratagem for bringing the Reverend back to the national prominence for which he so hungered—and thus propel him to the New Politic's presidential nomination. Finally, he contacted the Reverend to arrange for Sophia to attend his next staff meeting, to outline a plan that the Chairman assured him he would "enthusiastically endorse." After the usual introductory pleasantries, Sophia addressed the group.

"Gentlemen, I would submit that rather than discussing the 'what' of various issues, you should be focusing on the 'how.' To lure in more congregants, maybe it's not the issue itself that you should be thinking about, but the way to exploit it, to introduce and promote it. Perhaps many of the issues you've often reviewed would work. You just need to find some extraordinarily graphic way to grab the public's attention."

"So do you have an example?" someone asked.

"Actually, yes. And before you reject this out of hand, hear me out.

"Think about the unending, unresolved problem of drug cartels, and the kidnappings associated with them, usually for extortion purposes. What if Reverend Christian were the victim of such a kidnapping—"

The Reverend, whatever else his critics might say of him, was a man of often unerring, impulsive imagination, especially one ignited by his awareness of the Chairman's support.

He rose from his chair and began pacing the room. "I like it. I like it. I like it," he began repeating as a mantra. His associates had seen this behavior before, and knew it was a good sign. Moreover, he began humming *Onward Christian Soldiers*, which always happened when he was excited about an idea, pondering its implications.

"What if—" he said, extending Sophia's hypothesis, humming between words as he marched back and forth across the room, "What if I began to push the drug issue hard? I know I've done it before, but it's been dormant for awhile, and the timing might be right to hammer it again."

Sophia quickly built on his line of speculation. "Yes, and let's suppose you leak that, as a result of your anti-drug crusade, you're getting threats against your life. And then you're kidnapped."

She now spun out a scenario that was the plan the Chairman had devised. The Reverend's humming was reaching a fever pitch. *Marching as to war, with the cross of Jesus, going on before.*

One associate, slower than the others, uttered, "Reverend, we should think about the risk you would take being kidnapped."

Sophia stopped him immediately. "It wouldn't be a real kidnapping. We'd fake it." Supportive murmurs filled the room. The Reverend rhapsodized, "Yes, yes, yes. Fake it. That's the ticket."

Sophia viewed Christian much as his critics did—a consummate coward who nonetheless paraded himself as one of God's avenging angels—but she had to acknowledge that he perfectly suited the Chairman's devices. After the meeting had ended, the Reverend ushered Sophia into his office. "So where does the Chairman want us to go from here?" he asked unctuously.

Sophia spent several hours reviewing a sequence of events with Christian. First, the Chairman wanted Christian to begin a series of sermons on his daily television show, lambasting the global drug culture. She underscored the importance of specific accusations.

"The Chairman insists that you name names, identifying countries and their leaders, being precise in your charges. This will intensify the inflammatory mood. Charges and counter-charges will likely ensue, which will raise the profile of the dispute. The Chairman will make certain that every one of his media outlets eagerly describes the punches and counter-punches. Once there has been sufficient tension generated, we can move on to step two.

"Which would be an explicit threat," she explained. "The Chairman will have his media leak that more than one prominent South American drug lord is calling for you to be silenced. We would identify them by name, and focus the accusations. The Chairman's view is that although drugs have grown into a vast global business, with Afghanistan and Mexico as key parts of the supply chain, for example, South America remains the center of the drug trade."

"How does the Chairman contemplate pulling off the fake kidnapping itself?" the Reverend asked.

"We will need to work that out, but don't worry; you know

how careful the Chairman is, and how many strings he can pull. I will be able to make direct contact with the individuals you name, or those who stand in for them."

It was at this point that Sophia fully described the New Politics plan, and the role the Chairman wanted Christian to play as the party's presidential candidate. The Reverend's mind was swirling; Sophia could practically see his neurons blinking like faulty lights on a Christmas tree.

*With the cross of Jesus going on before.* The Reverend sensed this was going to be God's long-awaited answer to his prayers.

What the Chairman had shared with neither Sophia nor Traveler—what he had, in fact, shared as yet with no one else—was his complete vision for the brave new world he would create and control.

The Chairman intended to use Colombia's drug lords not only to execute the fake kidnapping, and become part of an integrated cocaine supply chain—but to have them subsequently force Colombia's leaders and populace into becoming part of the Chairman's new "United States of the Americas"— actions precipitating a truly unprecedented tumbling of South American political dominos.

❖

Traveler had reported to the Chairman on Conman's suitability as a vice presidential candidate, and since then had received no further instructions from the island compound.

So after his museum meeting with Sophia, but before heading to New York in search of a place called the Flamingo, Traveler took a break with a weekend in Havana.

Havana had been Traveler's favorite hideaway for decades. It was a place where he was least likely to be recognized. Before U.S. relations with the Castro regime had been normalized, before Raúl Castro's death, Traveler had enjoyed virtual anonymity. Now, even after the U.S. government had relaxed restrictions, and Americans had become regular visitors, a code of privacy still seemed to prevail. Perhaps it was a hold-over from the general paranoia that had long existed under previous dictatorships.

It was Traveler's passion for marlin fishing that had first brought him to Havana. The waters off the coast of Cuba provided some of the best fishing anywhere in the world, and despite the ocean's contamination, still attracted the most ardent anglers. Moreover, though Traveler was barely conscious of it, Ernest Hemingway's love of the island also influenced him. Traveler greatly admired Hemingway, who had been a practicing journalist himself.

Traveler was staying, as he typically did, at the Hotel Nacional de Cuba, on the coastal salient of Punta Brava. Now, sitting on his balcony, he stared contentedly out to sea, with the early morning sun beginning to break through the cloud cover. Yes, marlins were smaller and there were fewer of them than before, but a first-class boat, skipper, and mate continued to always be available to him.

Shifting in an antique chair, Traveler reflected on the Lincoln Memorial case. For starters, shouldn't they be pursuing more leads? Before the attorney general had essentially ordered the embracing of Islamic terrorists as culprits, the FBI and D.C. police had received hundreds of tips. And there were other aspects to the case that Traveler felt were being ignored.

In the final analysis, however, as he savored his freshly brewed coffee, with gulls scouting for breakfast and gliding in large circles overhead, Traveler felt he had no other immediate alternative than a steadfast recommitment to the investigation—biased and distorted though it may be. Despite his apprehension about the attorney general's motives, as a born-again Christian he had been taught that there was God and there was Satan, good and evil. There should not be room for ambiguity.

Traveler finished his coffee, rose from his chair and headed to the kitchen for a refill. The rooms of his top-floor suite were suffering from neglect, with a hodgepodge of Art Deco, neoclassical and neocolonial furnishings. But the suite was enormous, nearly eighteen hundred square feet. Built in 1930, every manner of celebrity had stayed at the once-proud hotel in its heyday: Frank Sinatra, Ava Gardner, Errol Flynn, Hemingway, of course, even Winston Churchill. In the late 1950s the hotel was purchased by some of America's top underworld figures who had been living in Havana. The face of organized crime had changed greatly since then, but a few members of the old criminal clan still remained. Traveler knew them all.

He returned to the balcony, musing on the fretful dream he had had the night before. It had been bizarre, almost comical. He was at the helm of a large boat that had been loosed from its moorings, drifting along a river. Though he was in the captain's seat, he knew neither how to steer nor stop the vessel. The passengers were members of some sort of exclusive club. They apparently met regularly, and a meeting was now taking place on board.

A particularly noteworthy passenger was a gentleman who, in his prime, had dominated every room he had ever entered; he was addressed as "Governor." Once irrepressibly zestful, Governor's sunny disposition had become clouded by dementia.

"I was back in the Oval Office," he said to his fellow group members. He robotically uttered phrases that bespoke a world removed from the generally accepted notion of reality. "I spend most of my time there these days. I thought the secretary of defense looked good. Our weapon is faith. God will lead us in a mighty crusade. We must never succumb to moral compromise." The Governor's persona seemed to fragment further. "It is time to crawl out from under the pews. To stop contemplating spirituality through stained-glass windows. We've had enough talk. To war!"

Whoever he had once been, he was no longer.

As the shipboard meeting progressed, Traveler stood alone at the boat's controls. The river was about to make an almost ninety-degree turn, and he was helplessly spinning the steering wheel in every possible direction—sensing a heart-of-darkness danger upriver.

Traveler scorned so-called Freudian dream analysis, but the meaning hardly appeared in question. Traveler was being severely tested by events; he prayed the person he thought himself to be would not be strained, like the Governor, to the point of identity diffusion, or even worse—complete fragmentation.

❖

The weekend over, Traveler returned to Washington, then left for New York by car, Savant at the wheel.

They would be working together to follow up on the incident Sophia had mentioned, involving the matchbook that had fallen from Jaffee's jacket at his apartment, the one reading "Flamingo, NYC."

Fewer people took to the highways these days, given the unpredictable roads; dodging potholes had become almost a national sport. Traveler had never enjoyed longer distance driving, and the constant detours made navigating the deteriorating freeways even more difficult.

It took them a good six hours to reach the outskirts of New York. They traveled laboriously on what remained of Interstate 95 to the northern entrance to Manhattan, the only one that remained passable. Then they jumped on Harlem River Drive, going south. They continued downtown, passing the Guggenheim Museum and the Empire State building, both in various stages of advanced disrepair.

Arriving at One Police Plaza, just south of the Holland Tunnel, Traveler and Savant signed in at the security booth in front of the building, fortified by a patchwork of barricades. They were ushered through several poorly lit hallways, into an open room with a warren of cubicles, and were finally seated at the desk of a New York City detective.

The detective dispensed with the usual niceties, and said, as if in the middle of some previous conversation, "Diversity, that's what this city has always had. Or, if you're more cynical, you might call it theft, murder, corruption, the tired, the poor. But I prefer the euphemism." Pulling on his mustache, he continued, "Law-breaking has become more brutal, yet paradoxically more sophisticated. We're actually in a war zone here. I miss the camaraderie between crooks and cops that once existed."

"I imagine we should get to the purpose for our visit," Traveler gamely interrupted. "As you know, we're part of a team working on the Lincoln Memorial murder case. As I mentioned over the phone, one lead involves a past patron of a New York establishment known as the Flamingo."

"Well, I've done a little research, and the Flamingo, I found, is no longer in business. Located in Harlem, it was demolished and replaced by a corner grocery. After our conversation yesterday, I ran a computer check on the place. Here are the printouts." He handed a thick sheaf of papers to Traveler. "Sorry," the detective said, although he didn't sound particularly apologetic. "Our computer system broke down again, so I couldn't put it on a flash drive."

The detective leaned back in his chair. "I discovered that Harlem's Flamingo was apparently a hangout for talent-challenged writers, druggies, and Gulf War veterans with scrambled brains—a kind of forum for endless debates and rants about the so-called burning issues of the day. The information you have there should list the names and addresses of previous owners, that kind of stuff, plus any arrests associated with the place. The only advice I can give is to just start digging through it…see where it leads."

Traveler and Savant thanked him, left the building, and headed for their hotel, to their respective rooms. It had been a long day, and on the way they picked up some Chinese food for the evening; both were ready to settle in.

Before calling it a night, Traveler picked up the pile of reports, flopped down on the bed, and began going through the printouts. He noted places to visit and people to contact. It was an eclectic list, but for cocaine possession and disorderly conduct arrests, one name kept appearing. After filling a page or so with handwritten comments, Traveler dozed off.

After breakfasting with Savant, Traveler thought he'd try his luck and called the Harlem phone number listed for the likely alias he had highlighted the previous night. He was actually surprised to hear a vaguely recognizable voice at the other end of the line say, "Yes, that's me."

Traveler succinctly explained that he represented Washington police, was investigating a murder, and following up on a tip that a now demolished saloon named the Flamingo might provide important clues. The contact said little, and seemed tentative, but agreed to meet for dinner at Harlem's Versailles, an old Cuban restaurant.

❖

The ambiance of the Versailles was not particularly to Traveler's liking. It was crowded, the walls were lined with garish rococo gilt-framed mirrors, and noisy tuxedoed waiters bustled about. There was nothing understated about the Versailles, but Traveler had heard it served the best Cuban food outside of Havana.

Savant accompanying Traveler, the men had agreed to meet at the front entrance. The contact had said he would be wearing a white carnation, though there was no need for the flower. Laughing and shaking his head in disbelief, Traveler immediately recognized him. It was Conman.

Savant whispered to Traveler, "Truly an imponderable situation, a conundrum wrapped in enigma, and nested in Russian dolls. But in this world of constant surprise—"

Ignoring Savant, Traveler greeted Conman, who said, his smile broadening, "I bet I'm the last person you ever expected to see. I immediately recognized your voice over the phone—and couldn't *wait* to see the look on your face."

Savant having been introduced, the three men proceeded to a table in the middle of the restaurant, took their seats, and ordered drinks. Traveler began with the obvious.

"Why are you in New York, under these circumstances, and how did you ever get involved with police at the Flamingo?"

"Ah, yes," Conman replied. "Well, we all occasionally need a little diversion. Just as I understand you escape to Havana, I come to Harlem. After running away from home, like you I went through an early phase, as a teenager actually, lost in the wilderness—which in my case involved spending considerable time at the Flamingo.

"I've never been able to quite understand it, maybe just pure nostalgia, but ever since those days I've kept the small apartment where I lived during that period—whose number you dialed. It holds such path-seeking memories for me. Chicago and Harlem—my twin ports in the storm.

"I began as an ardent member of the Nation of Islam. I had a poor childhood, as you know, growing up in Chicago, and the message of Elijah Muhammad and his converts resonated with my parents. They were the great-grandchildren of slaves, and had deeply felt the prejudices of White America. The message of racial pride changed me, and it was a part of the polemics at the Flamingo. Afterwards, I was able to attend college on an athletic scholarship, and to begin a life that has led to where I am today."

The waiter returned and inquired if the three were ready to order. Traveler recommended the *arroz con pollo*, the chicken and rice. "I hear it's a specialty of theirs," he said, "or if you prefer beef, try the *ropa vieja*."

After they had ordered, Thomas pulled from his jacket pocket a sketch of how Joshua Jaffee might have looked many years earlier. "Recognize this guy?"

Conman studied the photo from different distances and angles. "You mean from my days at the Flamingo? Well, perhaps. But remember, I was only a kid."

He rubbed his forehead, as if to massage his brain into action. "Yeah, the image I'm coming up with is this woman. She must have been his girlfriend or something. Now stay with me..." As if the three were going anywhere.

"I'm seeing an Asian-looking lady."

The waiter returned and silently placed their drinks on the table.

"Exotic in appearance. With long, jet-black hair."

"Do you have a name?" Traveler asked.

"Sort of. It was something like Dominique Amber,

Eleesha Desiree...I'm not sure. I think she had a lot of aliases."

Just as their meals arrived, Conman abruptly got up from the table. "Well, I'm afraid my little getaway must come to an end. Got to catch a flight."

"Aren't you going to have dinner?"

"Sorry, on a diet. *Arrivederci*. I assume this won't affect the Chairman's plans for me?"

Thomas nodded, "Of course not," and sat back to await the arrival of his *arroz con pollo* and a check for three.

Traveler's next call was to one of the aliases that Conman recalled, also listed in the police reports. His luck still held, and after explaining why he was phoning, the female voice on the other end said, "Yes, I understand. I had an extensive clientele at the Flamingo. I got to know most of the regulars."

"Wonderful," Traveler replied, genuinely pleased. "Would you be willing to meet with me to look at an artist's sketch of what the person might have looked like when you would have known him?"

"Sure, but I charge by the hour."

Silence.

"I'm jesting. These days I live off royalties and clip coupons. I will give you some of my valuable time, no compensation required, if you indulge me in a small matter. I love visiting the Statue of Liberty. Some of my early ancestors arrived here as virtual slaves, many to help build America's railroads in the West.

"Later generations got into the country like other immigrants, greeted by the Statue of Liberty. Call me sentimental, but I can't get enough of the place. How about we take the ferry over tomorrow afternoon and walk the grounds?"

"Great. The dock isn't too far from my hotel. And when I say hotel, I'm not suggesting anything extracurricular."

"Not amusing," was her retort. Then she hung up.

❖

The Lincoln Memorial case had developed enough intrigue, Traveler thought, that there might be a book in it, or, at the very least, perhaps a lucrative high-profile series of articles.

So he took the opportunity to visit New York's Islamic Cultural Center, several blocks northeast of Central Park, to hopefully gather some useful local color or background information.

The Islamic Center was built of yellow and pink stone, a large copper dome perched on its roof, now tarnished like so much else in every American city. A lone, elegant minaret, detached from the main building, reached to the highest point on the mosque grounds. Crescent moons, symbols of the Islamic faith, stood atop both the dome and minaret. Traveler entered the main building and found himself in an immense open space, bathed in natural light, surrounded by walls decorated with elaborate but discolored ceramic designs.

It was Friday, and a throng of the faithful was attending prayers. He listened as the imam began speaking. The Cultural Center often attracted those who were not currently of the faith, but interested, or at least curious, so the imam took a moment to address the concerns of non-believers.

"We Muslims," he intoned, "are no longer pillaging Middle Eastern tribesmen. Islam is a complex, highly intellectual faith, and the Cultural Center embraces the many varying sects and divisions within Islam. Ours is, in fact, a diverse ethnic and racial religion. Black, white, European, African, Asian.

"Let me speak today specifically about the Nation of Islam, which seeks to combine black nationalism with Islam, and has its philosophical roots in Sunni Muslim teaching. Its founder, Elijah Muhammad, preached that 'the greatest enemy a man can have is fear.'

"I do not wish to offend, as I know that some of you do not share our beliefs, but I see fear-mongering in the behavior of the followers of other faiths, many of them Christian. An internal struggle often confronts African-Americans in this country, a tension between Islam's claim to brotherhood, and the stark reality of the black man's more than three centuries old experience in this land."

He shared his perspective for another five minutes or so, and brought his remarks to a close. "Let us pray for us all, and for a just resolution to the many difficult challenges before us."

# CHAPTER EIGHTEEN

**Later in the day**, Traveler and Savant arrived at the Statue of Liberty's ferry embarkation point. There they met a stylishly dressed, middle-aged Asian woman, with silky black hair reaching to the middle of her back. She introduced herself as Daiyu, and though no one had asked, she explained, "It means 'black jade.'" Traveler responded with an uncharacteristically gallant, "Perhaps you were named for your beautiful hair."

They headed for the Statue of Liberty office, purchased tickets, and boarded the ferry for the seventy-five minute cruise, heading to the prow of the open deck. "As I said over the phone," Traveler began, "I asked to meet with you to see if you could remember anything about an individual possibly linked to the Lincoln Memorial incident."

"You must understand," Daiyu said, her voice hard, "that I've met a lot of men in my line of work. They have become a blur to me, as a consequence of both time and intention." Then her face relaxed, and she said almost playfully, "If you were to show me a conspicuous, normally concealed body part, however, or a unique birthmark or tattoo…" Traveler handed her the drawing of Joshua Jaffe. "Do you remember this man?"

"I believe I do. A car salesman I once knew. He described himself as selling vintage classics, foreign jobs mostly—felt you dealt with a better class of people that way. I don't think he worked very hard at it, though."

As spray from the bow covered the threesome in a fine mist, Daiyu said, "A brilliant gentleman, as far as I could tell. He liked to ramble on about various theories of psychology." Savant gave indications Traveler recognized as wishing to elaborate on the topic's "various theories," so he raised a hand to cut him off. The ferry churned through the choppy waters. Traveler looked out at the New York skyline and panoramic view of the river.

"His talk about identity was intriguing. For an Asian woman like me, born in the Islamic faith, although obviously I've strayed far from many of its precepts—identity is a weighty matter."

The boat reached Liberty Island, and the trio disembarked and walked to the Statue's now vandalized, graffiti-covered observation deck. Traveler was preoccupied, trying to make some sort of connection between Joshua Jaffee and the apparent earlier incarnation Daiyu was describing.

"When he would really get wound up, he'd babble on about seeking freedom, riding like the wind," Daiyu continued. She grinned, "Of course, as far as I knew, 'riding like the wind' had to do with his passion for horse racing. I can't tell you the number of hours we spent at Aqueduct and Belmont Park."

'Riding like the wind'…where had Traveler heard that expression before? Ah, yes, in the so-called "poem" discovered in Joshua Jaffee's desk at the post office.

Daiyu gazed off into the water, perhaps straining to hear the echo of thundering hooves long ago; then turning suddenly to Traveler, she said, "In fact, indulge me further; take me to Belmont tomorrow, subsidize some modest gambling, and I'll tell you more."

❖

Traveler and Savant picked her up the next morning, and they left Manhattan with Savant driving east to the Cross Island Parkway, and finally south to Belmont Park. Along the way, he offered a brief historical observation. "Did you know that Belmont was first opened in the early 1900s, and its mile-and-a-half track was once the largest dirt course in thoroughbred racing?" Neither of his fellow passengers seemed interested.

Once parked, the threesome strolled towards the grandstand. They seated themselves before a green infield dominated by two lakes. Though the trees around the track's periphery had died, gambling still paid Belmont's owners enough to keep the lawns looking fairly lush. Games of chance, like drugs, seemed immune to economic upheaval.

Traveler was still trying to reconcile the mild-mannered, stoop-shouldered post office employee—with his apparent alter ego, a psychology-theory-spouting horse racing addict. "You don't remember his name, by any chance?" Traveler asked.

"Actually, no. Most of my clients never gave me their real names, anyway. And I was so completely in the thrall of his entertaining companionship that his name was of no consequence." Traveler mused that he doubted anyone had ever described Joshua Jaffee as particularly "entertaining."

"Did he have any enemies that you were aware of?"

"None that come to mind. I think he won more than he lost, so maybe he wasn't too popular with the bookies and track owners. He said that his winnings paid for things like the sports jacket he always wore. It was a very expensive designer affair. Called it his good luck charm."

"Isn't that the kind of jacket they found in Jaffee's—" Savant began. Traveler again raised an imperious hand.

"I'd hear him talking to himself sometimes," Daiyu continued, "in what sounded like some kind of angry dialogue. He kept using words like 'payback,' like he owed something to someone."

It was the end of the racing season, and that day the wagering gods failed to smile on Traveler. Savant and their companion met with considerably more success, though their methods for betting diverged greatly. Savant went through regression analyses of horse lineage, past racing conditions, and jockey records of success. Daiyu's betting seemed purely random.

When the highest-stakes race started, the favorite took the early lead, with the crowd and Savant roaring their approval.

Down the stretch, however, the horse suddenly went rubber-legged, and a long shot nipped him at the wire, netting Daiyu five hundred dollars on her ten dollar bet.

"But the favorite couldn't lose. All the data said so," Savant moaned as he and Traveler accompanied Daiyu to collect her winnings. As she prepared to hand over her ticket, holding it in front of her seemed to elicit a memory. "Oh, yeah, there was what I thought of as useless old pieces of paper he collected. I never saw these stamps, but he'd rave a little from time to time about what I believe he called his 'airmails.'"

# CHAPTER NINETEEN

**The Chairman** had several South American contacts in mind for his kidnapping caper. Actually, "caper" was far too frivolous a word to describe the implications he envisioned for an event he hoped would serve as the catalyst for an earthshaking chain reaction—involving two continents, if all went well.

The Chairman's thirst for control was insatiable, but it grew not just from a grotesquely inflated ego, but a deep insecurity. To the degree that he could tightly manage his world—perhaps *the* world—the Chairman felt safe. From his vantage point, like distorted images in a funhouse mirror, threats existed everywhere. He acknowledged that his ability to regulate some natural events—hurricanes, errant asteroids, viral plagues—was still a little dicey.

Successfully manipulating people in large numbers, though, was much more achievable. The masses, after all, had long been swayed by myths, ideologies, faith: Christianity, Buddhism, Islam, Judaism; democracy, capitalism, socialism, communism, fascism; the list went on.

There were always crude methods of manipulation; the Chairman was fond of Lyndon Johnson's dictum, "If you have them by the balls, their hearts and minds will follow," but he liked to think he was capable of a tad more finesse.

The Chairman's insecurity was the principal reason for his mission to dominate global media. The medium was the message, and by controlling it, you controlled what the public saw, heard, and thought. He had also begun to envision an even shorter route to protecting himself from dangerous human forces—through the large scale sorting and rearranging of human neurons and emotional chemistry.

The development of *Matrix*-style technologies remained in the early stages, although the Chairman had been quietly investing more money than anyone else, individual or nation, in brain-based, drug-based technologies. Over decades, he had tightened his grip on as many parts of the Internet as possible, with an imaginative conception of someday connecting the human mind directly to what had evolved as a single Internet "cloud." A blended electronic and biological artificial intelligence was the ultimate nirvana.

Perhaps it was all futuristic mumbo jumbo, but in the meantime an arsenal of drugs—heroin, marijuana, cocaine, PCP, meth, LSD—could help govern consciousness. What was needed, the Chairman thought, was an organized way to make drug use legal, irresistible, and universal. He intended nothing less than an impregnable organization of all production, marketing, and distribution of drugs; in a seamless, vertically integrated supply chain.

❖

After carefully analyzing options for the best drug to achieve his ends, he settled on cocaine, as having the greatest addictive power with the fewest undesirable side effects. Cocaine would serve as a core ingredient in a blockbuster chemical cocktail the Chairman's army of chemists had created.

His plan was to make this chemical cocktail readily available, initially to each and every U.S. citizen, to make it as ubiquitous as water or toilet paper. Later, distribution would be expanded to Canada and, to the south, Mexico, Central and South America. His dream was to have the cocaine-based "medication" in every household, every pantry or bathroom, in every woman's purse or man's pocket.

Reverend Christian's fake kidnapping was intended to vault him to the presidency, as the media would spread the fiction that he had heroically escaped his captors, and would pave the way for the triumphant revival of his role as the preeminent moral values adjudicator. With the assistance of the Chairman's limitless network of influence peddlers, Reverend Christian would be lionized far and wide, and be elected in a landslide.

Pulling the strings behind the scenes—the Reverend Christian was his man, bought and paid for—the Chairman felt assured that he would be able to manage all cocaine production in the Western hemisphere, ninety percent of worldwide supply.

This needed to begin in Colombia with a small coterie of

drug lords. They would not only help put together his cocaine syndicate, but eventually spread the New Politics movement throughout South America.

❖

The traffickers in the two cities, Cali and Medellin, had been weakened over time, but remained at the heart of the cocaine industry. The Chairman had developed connections with Colombia's patrician class, starting with the country's president, whose corruption was legendary. Meetings had been arranged in Cartagena, Medellin, and Cali.

The Chairman had assigned the liaison task to Sophia, after she had completed her visit with Reverend Christian. The Chairman was confident that, to successfully negotiate the most complex and delicate of matters, no one was more qualified than Sophia. She would need the agility to interact with both powerful politicians and ruthless drug lords. In the Chairman's mind, Sophia possessed the perfect blend of disarming innocence and calculating, unrelenting drive that was required.

She was unaware, however, of the Chairman's intention to actually control cocaine production, and was told she would be meeting with drug lords only to organize the fake kidnapping.

Thus, while Traveler was in New York, she found herself in Cartagena, in the land of the legendary city of El Dorado, cocaine barons, and a seemingly inextinguishable guerrilla insurgency. Indeed, a mixture of extreme poverty, fabulous wealth, ancient culture and criminal enterprise prompted some to jokingly call Colombia "Locombia," the mad country.

Cartagena had been a major outpost of the sixteenth century Spanish occupation, encircling itself with an elaborate system of walls and forts. Located on the northern tip of Colombia, it had miraculously escaped not only the ravages of previous centuries, but much of the global destruction in more recent times.

Sophia was to meet the country's president in her suite at the Hotel Charleston Cartagena, once a meticulously restored destination for international travelers. At the appointed hour, she was surprised to open the door and greet not only the president, but the leader of Colombia's Catholic flock, as well, the cardinal.

"Ms. Sophia, I have taken the liberty of inviting His Excellency, the cardinal, to our session today," said the president. "I hope that I have not overstepped my bounds."

"Not at all," she assured him. "I appreciate your initiative." Seeing them together, apparently congenial and intimate, she began to assess whether the cardinal had also been drawn into the web of corruption that engulfed Colombia.

As if answering her unspoken question, the president announced, "We have become comrades in arms, converts to *realpolitik*. Living in Colombia makes that essential."

The cardinal took up the discussion. "Ms. Sophia, as you

may know, our social stability has long been jeopardized by guerrilla groups of a variety of persuasions. We must contend with both leftist rebels and right-wing paramilitary forces. Our country seems in a state of constant civil war."

"Yes, gentlemen, and I know I speak for the Chairman here, we appreciate the many afflictions you bear," she said sympathetically. "I hope that what we are asking of you, and what we are offering in exchange, will help to partially alleviate those burdens."

She proceeded to outline the Chairman's intentions, explaining that in the near future an "event" would be staged that would involve the participation of important Colombian cocaine barons.

"Meeting with them will be the purpose of the remainder of my immediate stay in Colombia. After receiving your assurances that neither the Colombian government nor the Church will interfere with our efforts, nor aid those who might attempt to do so, I am authorized to proceed to Medellin and Cali to discuss the Chairman's plan with potential partners."

What she said next drew her listeners' full attention. "In exchange for your cooperation, the Chairman is prepared to have five hundred million U.S. dollars deposited in each of your names, in whatever accounts you designate, to be used in whatever manner you choose." The Chairman so trusted Sophia's cunning judgment, that he had permitted one billion dollars to be committed at her discretion alone.

The president sat bolt upright. "Let me understand. I want to make certain that there is neither error in translation, nor confusion over currencies. You said five hundred million U.S. dollars?"

"That is correct."

"And please explain further what we must do to justify that sum of money," the cardinal said skeptically, folding his arms across his chest.

Sophia was not in the least unnerved. "The Chairman simply wants your personal pledge—with my validation—that you will use all the influence at your disposal to make certain, when the event to which I have referred takes place, that neither Colombia's political nor religious constituencies will interfere.

"For such assurances, the Chairman will have one hundred million dollars immediately deposited in your names as a token of our good faith, with the remainder deposited at the conclusion of the event."

"Señorita," the president said, "are you able to provide some further indication of what types of interference the cardinal and I might expect?"

"I will try," she said. "The event will receive international attention, and you will most certainly be asked to use Colombia's internal forces to direct the outcome. The Church in Rome and the United States government will pressure you to intervene, but we will expect that your influence will be vigorously exercised to thwart such intervention.

"If, after we make you aware of the full details of the project, you are not comfortable proceeding further, you may each keep the initial one hundred million dollars, without further obligations. Understood?"

The two exchanged glances. Through their many years of sometimes fractious collusion, they had learned to read each other without conversation. Both gentlemen nodded, and the president spoke. "The cardinal and I agree to your terms." Exercising her intuitive skills, Sophia appraised their agreement to be genuine and reliable.

With the business at hand concluded, the president departed, citing pressing matters of state. The cardinal remained briefly, asking if Sophia's schedule permitted her to spend a few hours with him the following day.

❖

The next morning, she stood on the steps of the Iglesia de San Pedro Claver, a mile or so outside of Cartagena.

"Thank you for coming, Ms. Sophia," the cardinal said, as he emerged from the church to greet her. "Please, walk with me."

They entered the door beneath the church's imposing facade and walked towards the high altar. "I wanted to explain my position and that of the people of Colombia, for whom I am a shepherd. You may choose to accept what I say as sincere, or not, but I felt the need to at least share with you my thinking."

"Yes, of course."

"This particular church," the cardinal said, "is dedicated to the memory of the Spanish-born monk, Pedro Claver. He lived and died in the convent adjacent to this building, spending his entire life ministering to the slaves brought from Africa. That, Ms. Sophia, is the tradition of service to others upon which my work in Colombia has been based.

"The Catholic Church, here in South America and throughout the world, has come under enormous criticism in the past century. We have been called insular and selfish. I will only submit that nothing could be further from the truth, at least in Colombia.

"I do not know with whom you will be speaking in Medellin and Cali, but I can guess, and in doing so suspect that, for these individuals, whatever else their motivations, the welfare of the poor in our country will not go unrecognized."

He turned to her. "With your indulgence, I would like to show you one other place in Cartagena that is important to our culture."

Leaving the church, the cardinal escorted her to his car and instructed the driver to take them to the Castillo de San Felipe de Barajas, built in the mid-1600s. They drove beyond the outskirts of Cartagena's old town, and stopped at a huge fortress perched on a hillside overlooking the city and harbor.

They got out and stood alongside its massive stone walls, Cartagena and the sea spread before them. The cardinal picked up his conversation where he had left off.

"When the conquistadors first arrived here, they slaughtered or enslaved the indigenous native tribes, and then made Cartagena the treasure city of the Spanish Main, with this fortress the site of much cruelty. Thus began a tradition of greed and corruption in this country.

"Many of us oppose those who oppress Colombia's common people. My portion of the money that the Chairman has been so gracious to offer will go directly to my country's poor. I simply wanted to share that with you."

Sophia was skeptical, and would report back to the Chairman that he should anticipate the cardinal's five hundred million dollars to be spent on nothing other than funding an additional wing to house the Vatican's surplus of gold goblets.

# CHAPTER TWENTY

**Sophia watched** from the window as her aircraft descended, the city of Medellin growing larger. She looked down on the spectacular landscape of the Aburra valley, offset by the vast slums blanketing the surrounding slopes of Colombia's second largest city.

She had met with the president and cardinal, and believed she had successfully negotiated their support; now she was pursuing the same outcome with major drug barons in Medellin and Cali.

For more than fifty years, the centers of the cocaine industry in Colombia had been these two cities in the western part of the country. Each had developed its own business practices; Medellin managed its commercial enterprise through terrorism, whereas corruption had become the hallmark of the Cali cocaine region.

As Sophia's plane landed, she ruminated on her doubts about the Chairman's assignment; these concerns rarely left her mind. Again, and inevitably, however, his near omnipotence trumped any ambivalence—she was in too deep to back out.

Medellin's infamous past was, Sophia knew, linked to the legendary cocaine kingpin Pablo Escobar, who was finally killed after the Colombian government, with significant U.S.

help, had waged an intense anti-drug military campaign. The Chairman, choosing his allies obviously for their utility, not their ethics, had decided that, if he were to align himself with anyone in the Medellin area, it would be Escobar's successor. This was the man Sophia was about to meet.

As she collected her bags, Sophia was somewhat surprised to see the man in question at the airport. Although he was accompanied by three stolid, burly escorts, evidently he felt so assured of invulnerability on his home turf that he came and went in public as he pleased.

"Welcome, Señorita. You are even more beautiful than reported," he said. He was himself an aging but handsome man, she noted, with shoulder-length hair of a striking platinum-blond, even more unusual in a land of *morenos*.

Linking his arm in hers, he escorted Sophia out of the building to a waiting limousine, flanked by two other black limousines, lined end to end. A uniformed driver jumped from the car, and with a grand gesture opened the door for her. Black-tinted windows kept prying eyes from seeing the occupants of any of the three vehicles.

They drove to what Sophia's companion described as his main residence. The trip proceeded without interruption, the driver blithely ignoring stoplights; at each intersection, the lead car would stop and ensure that traffic came to a halt.

Their destination, on a hilltop overlooking Medellin, rather than being a single structure, was a palatial estate. They had arrived at the prison to which, for a brief period, Pablo Escobar had been banished.

Prison, however, was a misnomer. Escobar had transformed the original Spartan living quarters into a lavish five-star resort. A spectacular restaurant, with entertainment lounge, had been installed. American entertainers often made transcontinental trips to visit. Camouflaged cabanas, constructed uphill from the main building, made excellent retreats. A staff of chefs prepared each meal. In fact, once the restaurant and entertainment lounge were completed, Escobar regularly hosted parties, even wedding receptions. The Colombian government's prison guards became no more than Pablo's employees, with Escobar's vehicles simply waved through military checkpoints.

"You have perhaps heard of this place?"

"Most assuredly," Sophia said, adding facetiously, with rare uncensored spontaneity, "It's regarded as one of the seven wonders of the drug underworld."

"I appreciate the humor, Ms. Sophia. May I show you around?" She nodded, and they set off on a tour of the grounds.

"Pablo Escobar was misunderstood by much of the world," he began. "He was firm, but always just in his decisions, and a true business genius. The poor people of Medellin enjoyed happier times when Pablo Escobar was alive.

"He identified with the poor, especially the people where both he and his wife were born, a small village northwest of here. These people, as well as his family, adored him. On his forty-second birthday his mother, wife, and children gave him two Maoist caps, which Pablo wore and adopted as his trademark. 'I will be like Che Guevara with his beret,' he would say. Che was his hero, along with others who led true peoples' revolutions.

"But I have talked too much, Señorita, and likely of things that are of little interest to an American. My excuse is only that I loved Pablo Escobar like a father, and as *my* hero. Perhaps you would like to rest before dinner. Let me show you to your accommodations."

He led her through several hallways to lavish, exquisitely decorated adjoining rooms. Leaving her at the door, he said, "Take some time to relax and freshen up. Dinner is at eight."

❖

That evening, Sophia sat down to dinner in a dining room festooned with flowers, which recalled a happy childhood in her family's English garden.

She had come a long way since then, she mused, to master, quite unexpectedly, the world's many intimidations; she was, after all, about to dine with a Colombian drug lord, one of the country's richest and most feared men.

"So tell me, Señorita, what precisely brings you to Medellin? I understand that we owe your visit to the Chairman."

"Yes. He extends his best wishes, and asks that you speak with me as if you were speaking directly with him. I believe that you have been informed to that effect."

"It is my pleasure to speak with you on that basis, Ms. Sophia."

"I have been privileged to meet with your country's president and cardinal before coming to Medellin," Sophia began. "They have assured me they will fully support the activity that I am about to describe for you. I am here to ask for your cooperation."

The first dishes in what would prove to be a magnificent feast now arrived: caviar, fresh salmon, smoked trout, asparagus salad, soon to be followed by an enormous roast turkey.

"This is a meal we reserve for only the most special of occasions. It duplicates the menu for Pablo's forty-second birthday celebration."

"I am honored," Sophia replied.

"You are most kind, Ms. Sophia, but I apologize, you were saying—"

"Yes, what the Chairman has requested is that you, as well as your associates to the south, in Cali, both participate in, how shall I say, a bit of theatre, perhaps. He needs you and your colleagues to agree to help stage, ah, a melodrama. You need not understand the objectives for staging such a melodrama, but you must play your roles with complete authenticity."

"I'm afraid that I am still unclear about what I am being asked to do," her companion said.

"I apologize for being vague, but this is a task that, at first consideration, can be difficult to contemplate in a sober vein. I assure you, however, it is most serious. What the Chairman needs you to do is to pretend to kidnap an important American clergyman by the name of Reverend Christian."

"Yes, I have heard of him. He is one of your foremost, how do you say, evangelical Christians. I believe that's the term."

"You are correct. Again, the Chairman's motives in this affair are of no importance. You need simply to understand that the fake kidnapping must be carried out flawlessly. The Chairman will provide you with a script for how you and your associates will report this kidnapping to the public.

"Furthermore, and I understand this might sound unusual, Reverend Christian will be participating of his own free will. He has his own personal reasons for cooperating, but he will shortly be launching in the United States a crusade against cocaine coming specifically from Colombia.

"He will be precise in his accusations, naming names, including yours. This will raise his visibility with the American media, and the Chairman will orchestrate a series of charges and countercharges. The result will be the alleged kidnapping of Reverend Christian, by what will be described as 'Colombian drug-smuggling terrorists.'

"To bring his crusade directly to the 'infidels,' as it were, Reverend Christian will arrange a meeting in Cartagena with Colombian dignitaries, including, of course, your president and cardinal. He then will proceed to Cali, where you and your associates will carry out the abduction. Ransom negotiations will ensue, arranged and organized by the Chairman. You must simply follow the directions you are given."

At the beginning of her soliloquy, Sophia had put down her knife and fork, speaking with an intensity that clearly conveyed the serious nature of the matter. Now she resumed her meal.

Her companion ate, without responding, for a few moments. He was impressed with how this beautiful woman could speak with such persuasiveness. Then: "I believe I understand what the Chairman would like us to do," he said. "And I am certain that my traditional rivals, the leaders of Cali's drug enterprises, will comply as well. However, and I don't mean to be rude—"

"You're wondering what's in it for you?" Sophia asked.

"As I said, I do not wish to seem impertinent, but to answer your question, yes, what does the Chairman envision as compensation for our help?"

"I'm afraid I cannot answer your question at this time. Only know that the Chairman has asked me to assure you that you will be more than amply rewarded—perhaps even beyond anything you could imagine."

Her companion was known as a shrewd businessman who drove a hard bargain, and someone with an arrogant disregard for his personal safety. But the Chairman's undisputed ability to eliminate those who stood in his way was more than sufficient to prompt assent.

He set his silverware down, rose from his seat, and moved toward Sophia for what she expected might be an awkward embrace. His smile had broadened, stretching his lips so taut it looked as though the corners of his mouth might crack. He took a few steps, and stopped. "Señorita, Señorita, if the Chairman wishes it..." was all he appeared capable of saying.

Sophia rose to meet him, responding, "I will take this as a 'yes,' then, Señor." The Chairman's faith that Sophia could charm and tame the most savage beast—had been merited.

❖

Sophia was soon on her way to Cali, the second narco-terrorism hub in Colombia, home to more than a dozen smaller groups involved in the cocaine trade. The Chairman had identified three brothers as most likely able to provide leadership for the so-called Cali Cartel.

Sophia was met at the airport by some of the brothers' minions. She was also met by Savant. He had shown up at the airport at the behest of the Chairman, who wanted both Sophia's and Savant's assessment of a nearby major cocaine growing and processing facility. Savant was scheduled to depart directly after the tour of the facility. Sophia would go on to meet the brothers at their hacienda, about fifty miles northeast of the city.

The minions ushered Savant and Sophia into a spacious four-wheel-drive vehicle, and they set off into the countryside.

Sophia enjoyed the ride, passing sugar cane and cotton plantations, and fields of tropical flowers, exported to the U.S. for those few who could still afford such luxuries.

She and Savant traversed a variety of guarded checkpoints along narrow, rutted roads. As they arrived at the cocaine facility, they were greeted by the manager, who asked them to join him in his small jeep. Once on the road, the manager began his tour. "What you will be seeing is an early prototype for what will be the most state-of-the-art drug cultivating and processing operation anywhere in the world."

Savant broke in, picking up the commentary. "Yes, you see, the Chairman, in utmost secrecy, has been working directly with this facility's ownership on this venture. Advances continue in cocaine cultivation, but it is still very labor-intensive."

"And we intend to keep it that way here in Colombia," the manager sternly interrupted, "for reasons of political and social control. New methods in cocaine processing are indeed being developed, but our interest is in streamlining, but not eliminating the manual process." He and Savant were apparently not in complete accord on this point.

Savant looked at Sophia, raising his eyebrows skeptically, and took over again. "What you see here is a large field of coca plants, in rows three feet apart, now three to six feet in height." Workers were busy picking the leaves by hand.

"Colombia's growing conditions cannot be adequately replicated artificially or synthetically—and although coca plants are found in other parts of the world, those containing strains of the highest alkaloid are only found here."

Savant also now knew, but refrained from mentioning, that cocaine's alkaloid would serve as a critical core ingredient, but not the only ingredient in the Chairman's ultimate chemical cocktail.

As they rode on, Sophia saw trucks taking the coca leaves to a line of immense low-roofed buildings. Cameras were everywhere. All activity within and around the buildings was under extreme surveillance.

The manager gestured towards the buildings. "The conversion of the coca leaf into coca paste or cocaine base is a delicate process. There are no other laboratory facilities anywhere that monitor temperature, humidity, and other conditions as rigorously as here."

Savant was uncharacteristically close-mouthed for the rest of the tour, careful not to reveal any of the Chairman's additional plans for Colombia and the formation of the United States of the Americas—the knowledge of which the Chairman assured Savant only the two of them shared.

The Chairman had come to trust no one more than this person as enigmatic, in so many ways, as himself.

# CHAPTER TWENTY-ONE

**Savant returned** to the airport in a separate vehicle, and Sophia continued to the brothers' hacienda, a horse and cattle ranch that stretched for eighty square miles on some of the most valuable land in the country.

Sophia's interpersonal competencies would again be severely put to the test, as the three men who greeted her offered a sharp contrast to their single counterpart in Medellin. Where he was affable and casual, they were stiff and formal, looking more like bloodless bankers than some of the world's most cutthroat drug bosses.

They all spoke softly.

"Señorita," the tallest brother said, "it is our honor to welcome you to our modest dwelling. We will do everything we can to make your stay comfortable."

"Thank you. On behalf of the Chairman, may I say it is a distinct pleasure to meet with you."

The hacienda had been built by the Spanish in the eighteenth century. The brothers had refurbished it, adding guest suites, expanding the kitchen (which they filled with every modern convenience), and building an enormous fireplace that dominated the outer wall of the main living area, rising sixty feet to the ceiling.

It quickly became clear that the brothers' main preoccupation, aside from marketing cocaine, was the care and feeding of nearly two dozen Arabian horses. Behind the hacienda lay a beautifully manicured racetrack with an adjacent paddock, where Sophia could see a few of the magnificent animals peacefully grazing. Following her gaze, the shortest brother said, "Many of these exquisite stallions we have purchased directly from the Saud family."

Dinner that evening was a seven-course meal that lasted for several hours; late into the night, they sipped after-dinner drinks. The middle brother leaned back in his chair; it was time, finally, to address the matter at hand.

"Before we hear about the Chairman's proposal, we would ask your forbearance to permit us to offer a personal point of view, Ms. Sophia."

"Yes, of course," Sophia said.

"Cocaine, Señorita Sophia, has been badly misjudged. It is one of the few benefits afforded to the poor of a country like ours, providing our people a simple but proud livelihood. More importantly, its consumption offers relief from daily hardships. Ours is a country that has been besieged by violence, it seems to many of us, since the beginning of time. We, the so-called drug traffickers, I would suggest, are trying more than anyone else to defend our people—against a corrupt government, a greedy oligarchy of the landowning classes, a right-wing military, and revolutionary forces on the left."

"Thank you for those words," said Sophia, though in truth she was hardly persuaded. "Let me say that the Chairman wishes, for reasons he cannot yet disclose, to generously compensate you, and thereby your people, for help in his enterprise."

Then Sophia outlined the fake kidnapping, mentioning the Medellin organization that would also be participating. "Your government's political and religious representatives will not in any way hamper our activities," she reassured them, "but will, in fact, facilitate these activities. Much of this project remains in early stages of development, but we are certain of its success."

"We have no doubt, Ms. Sophia, and you may assure the Chairman that we will do our part. We will speak with those you have designated in Medellin, and coordinate our efforts to the last detail."

"Thank you, gentlemen. The Chairman knew that he could count on your help." The Chairman also knew, through various surreptitious reports, that Sophia's negotiations on his behalf had been an absolute triumph. As usual, he gave himself all the credit, for having the perspicacity to have chosen her for the assignment.

# CHAPTER TWENTY-TWO

**Traveler had returned** to Washington from New York a few days before Sophia flew back from Colombia. Within hours of her arrival, he called her.

"Thomas, what a pleasant surprise," she said. "I hope you're not calling on business," she laughed. He found her merriment enchanting.

"Actually," he mumbled, "I thought you might be interested in a trip tomorrow to Annapolis. I go sometimes on weekends to get outside the Washington bubble. Might you wish to join me? I know this is rather last-minute…" He was annoyed that he felt like a bumbling teenager.

"I'd love to," she said.

"Pick you up bright and early, say eight a.m. tomorrow?"

"That would be wonderful. The Saturday forecast is for sunny weather, Indian-summer-like, I guess, with temperatures in the high sixties. Maybe we'll get lucky."

Unmindful of any double entendre, Traveler agreed.

"Do you know where I live?" she asked.

"Yes, of course. I'm a world-famous investigative journalist, after all," he joked.

He went to bed as nervous as a high school senior the night before prom. When he woke up the next morning, he had decided that he would make this Saturday a point of no return, one way or the other, in his relationship with Sophia.

Though they had been acquainted a relatively short time, he felt their connection was deep and undeniable, as if they'd known each other in some other life. He wasn't sure if he was being overly melodramatic, but he intended to achieve some kind of resolution.

As predicted, that Saturday in late October was crisp and bright. Traveler drove his fully restored 1961 red Thunderbird convertible through the streets of Georgetown. When in its prime, the area had been a favorite center for restaurants, bars, nightclubs, and trendy boutiques.

Now, though still high status, Sophia's neighborhood had become something of a citadel; she rented a fashionable apartment in a gated, heavily guarded community in this once cosmopolitan extension of central D.C. After security checked with Sophia, Traveler drove to her place, and she appeared as he was halfway to her door.

"What a cute car," she said cheerfully, bounding down the steps. She looked lovely, of course, in faded Levis and a red blouse, with matching red flats and scarf.

Traveler pulled onto U.S. Highway 50 and headed east towards Annapolis. What had previously been about an hour's drive now took twice as long. Detours were omnipresent.

"Tell me about the car," Sophia said.

"I'm kind of a student of the 1960s in America," he began.

"I grew up cloistered in Alabama, and somehow became fascinated with that period's turmoil of assassinations, protests, riots. This car symbolizes that era for me, I guess.

"I don't enjoy driving that much anymore, but in the early '60s, from what I've read," Traveler continued, "a T-Bird convertible was one of those sports cars kids dreamed about. You must have ESP, dressed in red to match the car.

"You look quite smashing, by the way." Traveler feared he sounded awkward; but in his state of infatuation he found spontaneous conversation difficult.

"Thank you. You must remember that I am Persian, and we Persians are more, how should I put it…" She searched for the right words, and Traveler was delighted by her choice. "…intuitive, and, well…sensual."

Traveler took this as an opening to ask more about her upbringing. "Is it true that your family is from Teheran originally?"

"My parents immigrated to England, where I was born, in the 1980s, after the Shah had been overthrown and Ayatollah Khomeini took control. My father was from a wealthy, well connected family, and he had been sent to England to preparatory school, university, and medical school. After he became a physician, he returned to Iran to join the Shah's personal medical staff. After the Shah was deposed, my parents endured increasing hardships."

"It must have been stressful, leaving their homeland and having to start over."

"They were fortunate. My father spoke English fluently, and, as a physician, had the skills that allowed him to find work. We lived quite comfortably."

"And you personally, how did you fare?" He tried not to ask such intimate questions in a rushed sort of way.

"I had no problem with English life, and as I grew older I ingratiated myself with London's young aristocratic set. I ended up married, briefly, to a notable English politician. Shortly after the marriage ended, my father was offered a prized position with the NIH here in Washington, and we moved to the U.S. I attended Georgetown and majored in advertising. Although we had never been especially religious, I found myself involved with Georgetown's Islamic society, and somehow gravitated to the more mystical strains within Islam, to Sufism."

"You're not a whirling dervish, are you?" he asked cheerfully.

"Yes, I guess that is the Sufi ritual best known to Westerners. Sufi mysticism seeks a oneness with the divine through meditation, poetry, music, and dance—a holistic understanding of the universe. Not satisfied to worship Allah from afar, the mystic wants to encounter Him directly." She paused. "I don't mean to sound so didactic. And I just told you we Persians were not very religious," she said, laughing again.

"You may find this difficult to believe," Traveler responded, "but what you describe sounds in many ways like my own born-again Christian religious experience."

"That's interesting," she countered, "although, at least as I perceive the differences, the Sufi experience is more than a sudden feeling of religious intensity. To set out on the Sufi path is to undertake a long, hard journey, without assurance that one will arrive at a destination.

"But I obviously am no expert on your faith," she added quickly, "and this is awfully abstruse for a marvelous outing in a classic Thunderbird, on a gorgeous Saturday morning, with a wonderful..." She left the sentence hanging.

Ignoring Sophia's attempt to change the subject, Traveler said, "Perhaps my journey is not representative of the typical born-again pilgrimage, but I, too, have found it longer and harder than I expected. But you were saying..." Traveler was eager to learn more about her.

"Oh, yes. Well, after I got my degree, I took an entry-level position with a large advertising agency. Our family spoke Farsi as I was growing up, and I had also learned Arabic, so I was a natural to start working on various Middle Eastern accounts. These clients were the origin of what was to become quite extensive globetrotting." They drove on, reveling in the weather and early autumn colors. Then Sophia spoke again.

"The most trying time for me was after the death of my father. He was a very strong person, and my mother and I depended on him. After he died, I felt adrift. I doubt that I have completely recovered, even to this day." Traveler digested this information without responding, until they reached the outskirts of Annapolis.

The city had remained essentially a military outpost, so its infrastructure funding had not dried up, saving it from the decrepitude that bedeviled most cities. It remained safe, relatively well maintained, and a popular recreation spot. Traveler drove to Church Circle, where he parked the car. "Anything special you'd like to do today?" he asked.

"Simply sightseeing would be delightful. Being outdoors. The colors. The fresh air. The companionship."

"If you're up for the walk, I thought we could head for the Naval Academy, then move on to Market Square and the city docks. After that we can grab dinner if you like, and head back to Washington."

"Sounds perfect."

With that, they crossed the street and entered St. Anne's Church. "I hope churches don't bore you," Traveler said.

St. Anne's, established in the late 1600s, had a unique history. It had been demolished by fire, and rebuilt several times. They walked down the main aisle, admiring the stained glass and soaring ceilings.

"Imagine the people who have worshipped here over the generations," Traveler said. "I admire this place; it's kind of an embodiment of spiritual endurance and reinvention."

"The words of a born-again man," Sophia said without irony.

"That doesn't put you off, does it?" He tried to conceal any hint of desperation.

"Not at all. Born again. Christian. They're mostly names, labels. But tell me more about what it means to you, exactly, to be born again."

Traveler reminded himself about the importance of this day, stopped, and inhaled deeply.

"When I was in Bosnia in the 1990s, I witnessed a brutal massacre. In a small village, Serb soldiers rounded up more than two hundred Muslim men and every boy over age ten. They held their captives at gunpoint, in front of their families. Then they bound their hands and feet and tied them all together. They were like some poor defenseless insects, caught in a huge spider web.

"The worst was that a number of U.N. peacekeepers, who were watching the activity, just stood there. They didn't do anything, or even say anything. Finally the Serbs started shooting into the crowd, even throwing hand grenades. It was all part of their so-called ethnic cleansing."

Traveler paused momentarily, lost in the horror. Sophia waited calmly, and he soon went on.

"It's still almost too horrible to remember, even after all this time.

"I couldn't fathom how a fair and loving God would allow such things to happen, and, for a long time, I was mired in a struggle to find any answer for it. A few years later I stumbled into a Billy Graham rally, and finally understood that a man must, as the Bible puts it: '...be born again...be born of water and of the spirit' to 'enter into the Kingdom of God.'

"The last thing that I would want, though, is for anything to stand between our getting to know each other better," he added hastily.

"I, too, would not like anything to stand between us," said Sophia quietly.

They turned from the altar in St. Anne's, and walked out of the church. They headed east along College Avenue, past St. John's College, until they arrived at King George Street, and turned south, toward the Naval Academy.

The sky was a translucent blue, with a few tufts of white clouds high above. The sun was still on its mid-morning climb, and a light breeze was starting to build. They walked along at a brisk pace, with Traveler, feeling as though a burden was being lifted, jauntily handling his cane. To passersby, they looked like two people who had known and appreciated one another for a long while, savoring a day's respite.

Traveler glanced at his watch as they reached the Naval Academy; it was almost noon. "I usually wander around the museum for an hour or two, but I'm not sure it's your cup of tea," he said to Sophia.

"On the contrary. I'd like to share the time there with you."

The images Traveler encountered in the military museum

sometimes sparked frightening flashbacks. Others might have avoided the setting, but to Traveler it was imperative neither to surrender to, nor retreat from his inner demons.

A giant mural at the end of one large hallway had always been especially evocative. It depicted a fierce sea battle from the War of 1812, with sailors thrown overboard, frantically grasping for flotsam and jetsam.

Whenever he looked at it, Traveler found himself tightly gripping his cane. Was he drowning as well? Would his born-again crutch, his life preserver, keep him above water?

As the twosome walked the halls, pausing to read inscriptions and scrutinize battle recreations, Sophia sensed Traveler withdrawing into himself further and further.

After they left the museum, they walked to Market Square, had a late light lunch, then wandered the half-block south to the harbor, where hundreds of boats were moored. They walked up and down the docks, past work and tour boats, pleasure craft, visiting ships. The docks were at the heart of the historic district, where many of the city's original eighteenth century buildings still stood. They found a bench and sat in the sun, absorbed in the activities around them.

Sophia broke the silence. "What makes you so interested in boats?"

"I'm not sure," he said. "I grew up in northern Alabama, far from any large body of water, so maybe its absence stirred my fascination. All I know is that the first time I set eyes on the ocean, I was hooked. One of my real joys has become fishing for marlin off the Cuban coast. I get down to Havana as often as I can."

Before he knew what he was saying, he added, "You should go there some time."

"Perhaps I might join you."

A Navy band, likely giving one of its last outdoor concerts before the weather got too cold, quashed further conversation. They listened for awhile; then Traveler asked Sophia if she would prefer to head back to Washington or have dinner in Annapolis. "I know a good restaurant near State Circle," he said.

Sophia readily agreed, and they set off for the Treaty of Paris restaurant. The dining room was furnished in period style, and Traveler got them a quiet table for two in one corner. They ordered drinks, and Sophia asked, "What do you recommend? I mean regarding the menu."

Traveler was preoccupied with his thoughts, and without consciously deciding to, disregarded the question. "I'd like to tell you more about what being born again has meant to me," he said. There was a brief strained silence; then the waiter arrived, and they ordered salad, white wine, and crab cakes.

"I don't know why I insist on coming back to my religion; maybe I'm repeating myself," he said apologetically. "But the Billy Graham rally was such a turning point for me. When I walked into Madison Square Garden, I felt heavy, world-weary; I'd felt that way for years. It hardly seemed worth-while carrying on.

"And then, as if touched by a miracle, I was totally enthralled. I can still picture it. The radiant, smiling faces, thousands of them. The rapturous music, the music of angels. Dr. Graham's resonant voice, reverberating about the auditorium. His magnificent words. Redemption. Surrendering to a higher power.

"I was transformed. I went up to the front of the auditorium and accepted Christ into my life. I have tried to make Him a touchstone ever since."

Sophia listened thoughtfully. "I have faced my own personal crises," she said. "One believes there is good and evil in the world, and wants to do good, but I find that knowing what is good is not always so easy."

"So very true," he said, staring past her in a sort of reverie. "The first few years after I was born again, choices seemed much simpler than they do now."

He kept staring, as if into a vacant unknown. Then he reached across the table and gently covered her hands, folded on the table in front of her, with his own. He had not intended to be so bold, and quickly snatched his hands away. "I'm sorry," he said.

"Don't be," she replied. "I have deep feelings for you. Perhaps that has been obvious." Her words had become almost inaudible, as she left his gaze and dropped her eyes to her glass.

The waiter brought the salad, then the crab cakes, and they ate listening to the sounds of a jazz band from the tavern next door. After dinner, hand in hand, they went to the tavern for a few drinks.

As the music grew soft and melodic, Traveler said, "I'm not sure what's right or wrong here. My inner voice gives me one message. My heart seems to say something very different."

"I was brought up to, when in doubt, follow my heart," Sophia said. She took Traveler's hand gently but firmly. They stood up from the table as one, and walked into the late autumn air.

❖

The next morning, they woke up together in a room at the Maryland Inn, a nearby bed and breakfast. There had been no explicit discussion; everything had seemed to unfold naturally. After a leisurely breakfast, they headed back to Washington. Traveler steered his Thunderbird to Sophia's apartment, and escorted her to the front door. Standing outside, they shared a final embrace. "It was wonderful," he said.

"It could not have been more wonderful, Thomas."

# CHAPTER TWENTY-THREE

**Malik Hassan** was preparing an early Sunday dinner in his set of rooms above the Orpheum theatre. The menus were consistent from morning to noon to night. He stood before the stove's burner and poured popcorn into a pan, gently agitating it as he heard the kernels explode into fluffy white clouds. He buttered and salted them, and, after finishing the meal, spent the remainder of the evening reading a biography of F. Scott Fitzgerald; about ten p.m., he put down his book, and began a pre-bedtime snack.

Humming to himself, he took a bite from a Hershey's chocolate bar and a sip of Coke, and paused, cocking his ear. He thought he heard a strange noise; his brain processed it as human, though he wasn't sure why.

Who could possibly be paying a visit, especially at this hour? His circle of acquaintances was small. It had been months since even his sister had stopped by. Perhaps it was one of those policemen who had come to talk to him before. "Anybody there?" he called out.

No one answered, but he suddenly felt very afraid.

After midnight, without leaving a note or telling anyone of his whereabouts, he drove to New York City and took the first flight to Beirut. It was only after his arrival in Lebanon that Malik, checking a D.C. online newspaper, saw the news that confirmed his sense of foreboding. While he had been in the air, his beloved Orpheum theatre had burned to the ground.

Early Monday, Traveler checked in at D.C. police headquarters, heard about the fire at the Orpheum, and called the detective heading the case. "Nothing very suspicious here," the detective said matter-of-factly. "There was apparently an explosion, likely the result of a gas leak, faulty furnace, that kind of thing.

"We're assuming so far that Malik Hassan was killed in the fire, because neighbors reported that he rarely left the theatre. But everything was incinerated. We couldn't even find teeth to match against dental records. Looks like an accidental death as far as we can tell."

❖

Despite unrelenting pressure from the attorney general to solve the Lincoln Memorial case, by Wednesday Traveler had already decided to spend another long weekend in Havana, and he had asked Sophia to join him.

They arrived late Friday; at nightfall, they took a taxi from the Hotel Nacional to the El Floridita bar and restaurant in old Havana. Sophia was intrigued by everything Cuban. "The taxis seem a microcosm of the city," she exclaimed. The multi-colored 1980s and '90s automobiles were restored American cars with scavenged parts, as if the vehicles were cannibalizing one another.

Little had really changed since the passing of the Castro brothers. There was more Cuban-American trade, and more vacationers had somewhat revitalized the economy, but it was still an impoverished city.

Traveler liked the El Floridita because he could order its Papa Hemingway Special, a daiquiri made with grapefruit juice. Although the food was usually bad and the service disagreeable, Traveler never tired of the place. It didn't occur to him that this might not be the best spot to choose for introducing Sophia to Cuban cuisine. He was blinded by the appeal of the restaurant's history. Its walls were adorned with photos of Errol Flynn, Gary Cooper, Spencer Tracy, and even Fidel himself, each hobnobbing with Papa.

"So what do you think?" Traveler asked as they entered the restaurant.

Sophia took in the details of the room. "I can see why you brought me here, to pay homage to your lost sibling from a previous life."

Traveler looked at her, puzzled.

"Hemingway. You're so similar," she teased. Both men shared not only a physical resemblance, large frame and rugged good looks, but also an episodic irascibility, which Sophia somehow found endearing.

On Traveler's recommendation, they ordered the pork roll stuffed with pineapple and mango, and covered in mango sauce. Despite the meal's mediocre quality, Sophia seemed enchanted by the general atmosphere.

After dinner, Traveler stopped briefly to purchase rum and cigars before continuing to a local boxing arena. He was sharing with Sophia the activities he found pleasurable, small tests of their compatibility. So far, she was passing with flying colors.

He began unwrapping a cigar as they walked the few blocks to the club, called Kid Chocolate. "Smoking isn't good for you, sweetheart," Sophia said with mock disapproval. Traveler muttered mildly to himself, but loved her gentle chiding.

Traveler enjoyed the amateur boxing matches at Kid Chocolate. The club's name honored a famous 1930s Cuban fighter colorfully nicknamed the "Cuban Bon Bon." Kid Chocolate had won the world junior lightweight title to become a Cuban sports legend. He had boxed mainly in New York, becoming a popular draw at Madison Square Garden.

As the couple left the fight club at the end of the evening, their conversation briefly turned to the Lincoln Memorial investigation.

"Every criminal case that I've ever followed has its unique rhythm," Traveler said, "and this case is temporarily at a standstill. The latest development is the disappearance—apparent death, actually—of the Hassan son."

For the rest of the evening, his thoughts, and hers, turned to other matters.

❖

They spent Saturday fishing for marlin, leaving the hotel before dawn and heading for the Marina Hemingway, ten miles west of downtown Havana. There the boat reserved for him was moored, a first-class craft with a two-person crew that handled everything associated with the trip except holding the poles and reeling in the fish.

Greeted by the skipper and mate, the twosome accepted early-morning champagne and settled into their chairs. Soon they were joined by the boat's owner.

Some years back, after learning of Traveler's periodic trips to Havana, the Chairman had arranged for Adolfo, the owner, to meet Traveler. The two men usually fished together whenever Traveler was in Cuba.

An odd circumstance, Adolfo was one of the current U.S. president's two brothers, obviously the black sheep of the family. He had changed his name, kept a low profile, and few people had paid much attention to him, the Chairman being a significant exception.

Now nearly eighty years old, he walked with a shuffle, a mere shadow of what he was once alleged to have been: part of an international crime organization. Traveler had never asked, and the president's brother had never volunteered much about that part of his life.

"Ah, such a beautiful lady," Adolfo said as he cautiously made his way up the gangplank. Sophia held out her hand to shake, and he took it and kissed it with dry lips.

Soon the boat was beginning to make its way out of the harbor, and as it sped up and headed out to sea, Adolfo began speaking about his youth, as he often did.

"My brothers and I both grew up amongst the urban underclass, but have obviously taken very different paths. I was the oldest, and despite my mother's relentless efforts to dissuade me, I became an expert, as a kid, at betting on street-corner craps games. Smart enough, I guess, to eventually become boss of the guys I ran with."

A son of Jewish immigrants, Adolfo stood only a few inches above five feet. As a youth, however, he had developed a reputation as the toughest guy "pound for pound" in his Brooklyn neighborhood.

"I loved the noise, the energy, the simple pleasures of life in Brooklyn," Adolfo said to Sophia. He clearly enjoyed the attention of an attractive woman, Traveler observed.

When they had reached about five miles out to sea, the captain slowed the boat, and the mate, who had been preparing the bait, readied the fishing poles. The skipper yelled down something in Spanish; Sophia, Traveler, and Adolfo each took a pole, and the hunt was on.

Turning to Traveler, Adolfo asked, "So how is your murder investigation proceeding?"

"Not so well," was the reply. "There's tremendous pressure to get a certain kind of conviction. I'm beginning to think that my confidence in the current administration may be misplaced. Sorry, no offense meant."

"None taken. Every administration is ripe with hypocrisy, as far as I can tell. Take my brother, the president, for example. A born Jew who somehow successfully masquerades as a Christian disciple. I've never understood how he gets away with it.

"I actually knew Joshua Jaffee," he continued. "I remember when he first chained himself to the Palestinian embassy gates here in Havana. I became acquainted with him after that. We shared a devotion to the homeland, to Israel.

"Now nearing the end of my life, I have only one major regret. As I'm growing older, my Jewish heritage becomes ever more important to me, and in the past dozen years I've frequently visited the Holy Land. My final wish is to be buried there. The problem is that Israel's laws prohibit those from becoming Israeli citizens who have what it calls a 'criminal past, likely to endanger the public welfare.' This would seem to make my burial in the Holy Land impossible. I fear I am destined to take my last breath on Cuban soil."

❖

Sophia and Traveler passed the day without landing a marlin, but much refreshed, returned to spend a quiet, intimate evening together.

Sunday morning, gray and overcast, they had breakfast at Ambos Mundos, a once classy hotel whose claim to fame was fostering the initial writing of Hemingway's *For Whom the Bell Tolls*. Although rain was threatening, Havana's citizens were making the most of the day. Kites were flying in the Parque Maceo, shoe repairmen were setting up outdoor kiosks, elderly men sat across from each other, engrossed in games of dominoes.

The elevator at the Ambos Mundos had long since stopped working, so the couple took the stairs to the top floor, to an open-sided bar and restaurant with sweeping vistas of the city.

As they entered, they could hear raindrops hitting the bar's glass roof. It was the kind of gloomy morning that served as a proper setting for contemplating murder—and the Lincoln Memorial bombing was always stirring in the back of Traveler's mind.

He ordered pancakes drowning in syrup and butter to help energize his thinking; nothing like a good dose of sugar and fat to lift one's mood. "Sweetheart," Sophia admonished, "such large amounts of cholesterol to fill small arterial cylinders!" She tousled his hair affectionately.

But neither the weather nor the food sparked new insight into the Lincoln Memorial case, and the couple left for the marina, where they boarded a thirty-two foot sailboat, which Traveler would be steering. By then the skies had cleared, and, as the boat edged away from the dock, the only sounds they could hear were the rippling of water under the hull and the flapping of the sail catching puffs of wind.

Traveler was in the stern, at the tiller. Sophia sat in the center, in a white top and shorts, jauntily wearing the captain's hat he had purchased for her. As the boat came under his control, he looked at Sophia and basked in the warmth of her presence.

They spent the better part of the day on the water, and returned to the hotel in late afternoon, intending to drift into a luxurious siesta. Traveler's deepening drowsiness, however, was soon interrupted by the sound of his cell phone, the number for which was known only to a select few.

"Traveler," he answered; there followed a lengthy silence on his end, until he finally said, "Interesting. The most improbable of long shots, but I'll talk to you further tomorrow."

"Good news?" Sophia asked.

"It's a bizarre occurrence. Probably doesn't mean anything, be we've just learned of an attempted sale of Inverted Jenny stamps in London. You know, the airmail stamp with the plane flying upside down."

Sophia drew in her breath sharply. "Of course I know of the Inverted Jenny. My stamp collecting, remember?"

"Sorry. Anyway, the buyer, the owner of the largest collection of Inverted Jennies in the world, is a reclusive old English billionaire. He was invited to purchase what was described to him as 'a pane of priceless airmail stamps.' Though tempted, he ultimately contacted Scotland Yard, after concluding the deal was too risky.

"He reported that he had intentionally resisted the proposed offer so he could reach into his massive informants network, unparalleled in scope, to see if they'd be able to shed any light on the transaction. He was eventually informed that the vague hint of a rumor had surfaced—flimsy speculation actually—that a pane of mint-condition Inverted Jennies had been found by a Washington postal employee, who had been killed, and the stamps consequently stolen."

"This sounds too incredible," Sophia interjected.

"I know," said Traveler. "And it gets better. One of the Scotland Yard detectives involved in the case had been following our Lincoln Memorial investigation. He knew that a Washington postal worker had been murdered, and was intrigued by the slimmest possibility of some connection, so British authorities passed their information on to the FBI."

# CHAPTER TWENTY-FOUR

**Back in Washington** on Monday, Traveler brought Savant up to date on the latest Scotland Yard development. Savant immediately started free associating about possible links between the two cases, with preposterous scenarios. Traveler simply tuned him out, as he had learned to do, bid him goodbye and arranged to touch base again the next day.

That evening, Savant worked his after-dinner crossword puzzle. "Keeps the mind agile," he always said. Forty-two down was "the irritation a bee can cause," five letters. That one was easy: "sting." He scrawled in the letters in his childish handwriting and glanced at the next clue.

Then he stopped. That was it, he thought. A sting operation.

He was beside himself with excitement. He put his pen down (he always did his crosswords in ink), and eagerly called Traveler. Traveler listened patiently as Savant burbled on about his brainstorm. But for once, Traveler had to admit, Savant might just have stumbled onto something.

Tuesday morning, he relayed the idea to the attorney general. Given that they temporarily had no other leads to follow, the attorney general authorized Traveler and Savant to devise a means for spreading the word: That a wealthy American stamp collector was prepared to outbid anyone—anyone in the world—for what he understood might be the buy of the century.

Savant had the FBI search its database of unofficial operatives, those obligated to the U.S. government in various ways, some less than aboveboard, to find a putative buyer. As he examined the myriad details about each individual, his eyes lighted on the name of an African nation ambassador, residing in Washington, D.C., who apparently had a credible reputation as a stamp collector.

Traveler was able to set up a meeting with the ambassador at his embassy, invoking the name of a high-ranking FBI operative. It was an urgent matter, Traveler said, and once at the embassy he would "explain everything."

On Wednesday, Traveler met the ambassador at the embassy's front desk. "I appreciate your seeing me on short notice," Traveler said as he followed the ambassador into his office.

"I hope it's as important as it's been made out to be. I was forced to change my busy schedule," he replied curtly.

Traveler didn't hesitate being discourteous, because he knew the ambassador had already committed to doing whatever was asked; his shady past had left him no choice. Thus, annoyed by his display of self-importance, Traveler shot back, "Yes, well, first why don't you fill me in on the scam that got you into such hot water with our government."

The left corner of the ambassador's mouth twitched, betraying the slightest fissure in his armor of arrogance. "I'm afraid

I don't understand the need to go back over that ground. Now, would you please tell me what's so pressing?"

Traveler explained that he could expect to be contacted about the sale of valuable stamps, help finalize a price for the merchandise, and finally accept delivery of the stamps at his embassy.

But the ambassador balked. "How can I participate when I don't understand the big picture?" he asked petulantly.

"You don't need to understand anything, actually," Traveler countered.

His mouth now twitching alternatively at each corner, the ambassador heaved a resigned sigh. "Have it your way."

After Traveler briefly elaborated on a few other aspects of the case, the ambassador's irrepressible smugness resurfaced. Glancing at his Rolex, he uttered with distinct finality, "I'd love to hear more, but I do have another engagement," and exited through a side door, leaving Traveler to find his own way out of the embassy.

❖

That afternoon, Traveler and Savant settled onto a park bench along the Mall, the agreed-upon meeting place for a covert discussion with the director of the Washington Philatelic Society.

He had resisted their invitation at first, wishing not to get involved, but easily cowed in the face of authority, the director arrived promptly. He parked himself on a neighboring bench, close enough to Traveler and Savant so they could converse in normal tones. To the casual observer, they might simply be strangers having a banal conversation about politics or the weather.

"Let me say up front that we appreciate your cooperation," Traveler began. "You must understand, and I can't emphasize this too strongly, that you are to inform absolutely no one about this affair."

"Certainly."

Savant took it from there. "We need to contact a party whose identity is presently unknown to us, an individual we believe may be in possession of some very rare stamps. We can't be so obvious as to feature it on MSN's home page..." Savant's modest attempt at humor was lost on the director. "...so we need your counsel about how best to attract the attention of such an individual; perhaps, for example, through an unverified story of a wealthy collector prepared to outbid all competitors for one-of-a-kind stamps."

"Likely the best way to do this would be to use the National Philatelic Society's weekly e-newsletter," the director said. "Anyone with a serious interest in stamp collecting subscribes. We could place a query letter with my e-mail address along the lines you have suggested."

"Excellent," Savant said. "I'll get back to you with the

letter we'd like submitted." Then turning to Traveler he asked rhetorically, "If that meets with your approval, chief."

❖

At the end of the day, Traveler's phone rang. Picking up, he heard a female voice, introducing herself as Ehsan, Sophia's aunt. "We have not as yet met, but given how my niece has spoken of you, I felt it might be instructive for the two of us to become better acquainted."

Traveler knew that Sophia and her aunt were close, and he was pleased at the request.

"Yes, of course, it would be my pleasure."

"Would this evening, say eight p.m., be too soon?"

"Not at all."

Traveler arrived at Ehsan's apartment a little early. She invited him in graciously, and after urging him to take a seat in the living room, disappeared into the kitchen.

The room showed evidence of an auspicious past, with photographs of ornate buildings in exotic places, and elegantly attired people in the foreground. An autographed picture of the Shah of Iran was featured prominently on the mantel.

"I see you've noticed that photo," said Ehsan, returning with a teapot, cups, and a small plate of baklava. "It appears in very few places these days. There was a time, though, when it was everywhere in Iran. The Shah was in most ways a good man.

He certainly treated my family with great courtesy. Yes, he had his excesses, but what regime does not? I would suspect that, given the current state of affairs there now, elderly Iranians with long memories might choose to return to those days."

Sophia's aunt not only shared her niece's physical elegance, but her forthrightness, Traveler noted.

"But we are not here to talk international politics, are we? My niece has told me many things about you. Many good things, I might add. I wanted to see for myself. You can understand an aunt's interest."

"Of course."

"You see, our immediate family was very close. Sophia's father was a pillar of strength. His death was a great loss to us. As I'm sure you have gathered, Sophia is a very intelligent woman. She also has a strong work ethic and a very creative imagination; thus her career has progressed admirably."

Ehsan offered Traveler another pastry.

"I broach this next subject with some apprehension, Mr. Traveler, because it concerns my niece's personal affairs. Some might judge it inappropriate for me to raise them in this manner, but I feel compelled to do so."

Traveler lowered his cup and placed it carefully on its saucer. He gave her his full and respectful attention.

"You see, Thomas, if I may address you so..."

"Please."

"...my niece has an often hidden, very private, shy side. She has become skilled at presenting herself differently in her public interactions, as Americans seem to reward assertiveness. But her father was a great influence on her. And as hard as it was for me to lose my brother, his death had perhaps the most profound effect on her.

"'Worship' may be too strong a word, but she adored him. I have come to believe that she measures all men against him. He was not perfect, but he was fiercely protective of his family; ultimately, it was the only thing that mattered to him.

"I am telling you this because I sense that my niece sees those same qualities of strength and commitment in you. Men often misjudge her flair and energy as inner toughness. She has a personal durability, but it is tempered by a …how should I put it… a certain fragility, not suited to bend with the changing winds. I worry that one day a fierce emotional storm might break her. I think it is important that you understand this perspective."

Traveler had sat quietly during her extended remarks. "I deeply appreciate you sharing these thoughts with me," he said. "I can only tell you that I will never intentionally do anything to harm your niece. I think that I see her quite accurately, and I, in turn, have tried to represent myself to her with as much honesty as I know how."

"Thomas, that is all that I might ask. Thank you for coming. May Allah be with you."

## CHAPTER TWENTY-FIVE

**The sting operation** was progressing rapidly. The director's inquiry was quickly published in the National Philatelic Society's newsletter, seeking information about a "rumor in philatelic circles" that invaluable airmail stamps might be for sale.

An untraceable e-mail soon arrived. "This is no rumor. We have such stamps," it read. "If you know of an interested buyer, have him place a want ad in the Tuesday online edition of the *Washington Post* worded: 'Arabian stallions for sale, unique lineage,' followed by contact information necessary for our use."

Savant wasted no time having the ad inconspicuously placed on the website, giving the ambassador's name, phone number, and e-mail address.

Thursday morning, an anonymous response, much like the first communication, was e-mailed to the ambassador at his office: "To confirm your interest in stamp purchase, will call at exactly three p.m. tomorrow."

At three p.m. almost to the minute, the African ambassador picked up his phone to hear a computer-filtered voice say, "This is a recording. Do not speak. I have a sheet of one hundred mint-condition Inverted Jennies. Will call next Monday at nine a.m. to hear offered price, if you wish to purchase." Then the ambassador was left listening to the sonorous hum of the dial tone.

❖

That weekend, the FBI brought in the Philatelic Society's director for his opinion on the authenticity and value of the stamps offered for sale.

"I'm absolutely at a loss for words," he said. "This is astonishing. If these stamps are genuine, there is no way to determine their value except through an auction process."

"So the owners of one hundred Inverted Jennies would also be uncertain as to their value," said one of the agents. "What would you suggest as a viable offer?"

"Well, comparing the auctions of recent rare collectibles, paintings, jewelry, and this is pulling a number out of the air—"

Savant, in attendance, could no longer hold his tongue. "Well, if you consider auctions at Christie's and Sotheby's, still the two best-known auction houses—although there's Doyle, Shannon's, Swann, as well—but in any case Picasso's *Dora Maar au Chat* was sold for ninety-five million dollars— and Giacometti's bronze sculpture "*Walking Man 1*" for over one hundred million, although both were sold years ago—let's see, single Inverted Jenny stamps have gone for two to four million dollars in recent times, and then, of course, a block of four Inverted Jennies was sold for seventeen million dollars in 2021—and just doing the simple math, four stamps at seventeen million multiplied by twenty-five, to give you the equivalent of the one hundred stamps in a pane—"

"We get the point," the agent interrupted. "But back to you, director..."

"I'd say that the price might be bid up to more than five hundred million dollars."

"Oh, I think that's far too low—" Savant started.

"Thank you, director. We appreciate your time."

The director rose and left the room. The investigative team, still trying to take in the figure he had mentioned, sat stupefied.

❖

So on the appointed day, at the appointed hour, the ambassador said into the phone, "If the product is genuine, I can offer you five hundred million dollars."

"Don't worry, they're genuine," the voice at the other end said. "We'll be in touch," it concluded, and, as before, unceremoniously hung up.

The next phone call, as abrupt as the first two, informed the ambassador that the price was acceptable, and stipulated the time and place for the transaction. The seller—or sellers, no one really knew—concurred that the embassy, technically not on U.S. soil, was as safe as any location for the meeting; if anything went wrong, the buyer could theoretically claim immunity, the seller asylum.

The ambassador was told to limit all communication during the transaction; the fewer words the better. Further, he was instructed that he would be making an electronic transfer of the funds to an overseas bank account, in the presence of the individual delivering the stamps. That individual, greatly disguised, would be in contact with an accomplice during the transaction, to assure the transfer was completed.

Finally, he was warned that the stamps would be enclosed in a container in which would be embedded a small, but powerful and tamper proof explosive device. If the emissary was followed or interfered with in any way, the device would be remotely activated, destroying the stamps—and thus evidence of a crime having been committed.

The exchange was set for Monday evening. The embassy would be sparsely occupied, and the disguised seller and the ambassador could meet in private. The ambassador would be wired so that FBI agents and Traveler, stationed nearby, could hear whatever conversation might take place.

The security guard at the embassy reception desk called to tell the ambassador that he had a guest. The first sounds the wire picked up were rapid footsteps growing louder as they approached the ambassador, seated at his desk.

Then a gruff voice demanded, "Turn off the camera I know is installed." The ambassador obeyed, quickly asking, "I assume the package you are holding contains the stamps in question, but what's the purpose for the cell phone—" That was all the FBI agents and Traveler heard, as the seller had apparently activated an audio jamming device.

The stamp container was opened, its contents examined, and then resealed. The ambassador was warned again about the embedded explosive material. After he asked, "What information should I use to execute an electronic payment transfer?" the clicking of a computer keyboard ensued.

As the seller headed to the embassy exit, the FBI closed in. A small figure left the building, observed the agents, and muttered into the cell phone being carried: "Arabian stallion." A bright light flashed; the source was the ambassador's office.

The agents swarmed over the figure, but only Traveler immediately recognized who the agents had just handcuffed, despite the disguise. It was Malika Hassan.

# CHAPTER TWENTY-SIX

**The announcement** of the arrest spurred a media frenzy. It was just as had been suspected, the government reported: Islamic jihadists had been the perpetrators of the Lincoln Memorial murder. Mosques throughout America, especially in Washington, braced for the anticipated vitriol.

The attorney general was among the first to call Traveler and offer his congratulations. "You've accomplished exactly what we asked. My people are very pleased. God's will has been done.

"All that remains is to bring in a guilty verdict. Doing so will involve the president's staff, as well as perhaps other powerful agents that I'm not at liberty to name. In any case, we all need to make the strongest possible collective effort here."

For the time being, Traveler again reluctantly agreed to play the role asked of him. What he would not do is join in any celebrating. As the Lincoln Memorial case had progressed, Traveler had experienced his growing love for Sophia and had encountered a thoughtful Islamic community—and his born-again guideposts were receding into ambiguity.

Because of his previous association, Traveler was instructed to conduct the initial interrogation of Malika Hassan. He met her in the secure lower level of the FBI building, in a windowless room furnished only with the requisite institutional table and chairs.

"So what do you think this charade will accomplish?" Malika asked stridently, before he even had a chance to greet her.

"Excuse me?"

"Being in this small, barren room, with that idiotic mirror; I know your co-conspirators are behind it, glaring at us."

Traveler leaned over, rested his hands on the table between them, and said, "You may be right about the setting, but you seem to have the players confused. *You're* the one involved in an illegal conspiracy."

"Do you think me a fool?" she shot back. "Unless the Constitution or Bill of Rights has been recently rewritten, I believe that the 'innocent until proven guilty' restriction still applies."

"Actually," said Traveler, "this is an open-and-shut case. You were caught trying to sell stolen goods. We have the e-mails, recordings, all conclusive evidence. We searched your premises and found stamps taken from Jaffee's album."

Traveler was bluffing, and steamrolled ahead. "Your brother was also clearly involved, and he was killed for being untrustworthy. You detested Jaffee's religious grandstanding and your family's fanatical friends wanted him silenced. It all adds up."

Malika made a slow clapping gesture in mock applause. "You've got nothing but a bunch of phony allegations and unsubstantiated circumstantial evidence. Jaffee gave me the stamps you found in my apartment." Malika suddenly became talkative. "He gave me the stamps on impulse, I think. Although I'm embarrassed to admit it, I felt honored by the gesture.

"As to my appearance at the embassy," she said, "through a series of intermediaries I was offered fifty thousand dollars to deliver a package to the ambassador, no questions asked. If these Inverted Jennies, as you call them, even existed, you can't prove theft, and you can't tie me to the Lincoln Memorial bombing."

"Don't try to distance yourself from this crime. First of all, during the stamp transaction, you were using a cell phone to give a prearranged signal—"

"I was on hold, trying to clear up an important business misunderstanding related to my family's Arabian horse breeding business."

"Horse breeding business? We've got a dossier on you, and we haven't found anything remotely connected to that in your family background. You can't really expect us to believe such nonsense," Traveler retorted.

"Well, if you can't accept the truth, that's your problem."

"Not exactly. If a jury of your peers are resistant, it will most definitely be *your* problem."

Malika folded her arms defiantly, and made her final statement: "I'm not saying anything more without my lawyer present."

Detective Moab, among those assembled behind the mirror, had watched the interrogation with disdain. "Islamic jihad" was a rigid paradigm through which all data was being filtered, he thought. The Establishment would twist reality to get whatever answers it wanted.

The next afternoon, Traveler began a second interrogation, this time of the Philatelic Society's director. He disliked the man, but not sufficiently to explain what was to be a rather cruel cross-examination. He didn't fully understand his actions.

Unlike their earlier open-air, park bench discussion, this time the meeting took place in a soundproof room, also hidden deep inside FBI headquarters. Traveler wanted no witnesses, and was prepared, he knew not why, to take significant liberties with the truth.

Traveler got right to the point. "New findings have come to our attention that associate you with the theft of the Inverted Jennies."

"Devastated" would have understated the director's reaction. The accusation put his brain in gridlock.

"The source of our information, and the information itself, are unimpeachable. Your only hope at this point, director, is to tell me everything you know about this case." Was he unconsciously reacting to some of what repulsed Moab about the director?

The director gradually emerged from his stupor. Tonelessly he began to describe each event that had transpired in the preceding weeks. He couldn't recall much unusual about his conversation with Detective Moab. He did remember being impressed by his question about theme collecting.

"I briefly talked," he now said, "about the theme in Mr. Jaffee's collection, airmail stamps. He didn't seem at all surprised, as if he knew they were the source of the collection's value."

Like the most profound of "aha" moments, the mention of Moab's stamp-collecting expertise ignited in Traveler the rough outline of a theory that would connect the Inverted Jenny stamp sale and Lincoln Memorial murder. He *knew* there must have been a legitimate reason—an inspiration, as it turned out—for his decision to interrogate the director.

Traveler recalled Moab's rumored romantic involvement with Princess, one of Jaffee's few close acquaintances, whom Traveler had first interviewed at the crime scene. And if Princess had somehow gained knowledge of the Inverted Jennies, and passed this information on to Moab...yes, it might work indeed.

"You say the detective seemed well informed about Joshua Jaffee's airmail stamps?"

"Yes."

What had been an unexpectedly productive interrogation now took an unhappy turn for Traveler. He told the director to do something he was to deeply regret. In hopes of discovering additional evidence, he had the director produce his scheduler and go through his activities day by day for the last three months. The afternoon dragged on with mind-numbing monotony, until the director reached an entry that read, "Follow up on Ms. Sophia's request."

He told Traveler about Sophia's phone call regarding the airline ad campaign. The TV ad, as the director recalled, would center on an important event in aviation history; the event in question was the printing of the Inverted Jenny. He added that Sophia specifically asked him to provide the names of noteworthy owners of Inverted Jennies. At the top of his list, the director said, had been a reclusive billionaire living in London—the very same billionaire, Traveler recognized, who had contacted Scotland Yard about an abortive stamp sale, the information that had then been sent to the FBI and Washington police.

With a tremendous effort, Traveler remained expressionless. He had obviously learned so much more than he wanted to know.

"Thank you, director. That will be all for now, but speak to no one about this case. Your freedom depends on keeping our discussion today in absolute confidence."

The interview over, Traveler immediately drove to Sophia's apartment. She had him buzzed in at the gate, and he almost leapt out of the car as he pulled up in front of her apartment. He pounded on the door, and with a mixture of relief and dread, he heard her say, "I'm coming. I'm coming."

As she opened the door, he pushed past her, fiercely gesturing for her to follow him into the living room.

"What is it dear?" she asked, bewildered. "Please, tell me what's the matter?"

Traveler was pacing around the room in a state of high agitation. Gently, she walked him to the sofa and sat him down. He took her hands.

"Darling, you know I will always protect you," he said. "I love you, but I must seek the truth in the Lincoln Memorial case."

With a sinking heart, he saw Sophia's face tighten.

"I have just spoken to the Philatelic Society's director. I know you sought information about the Inverted Jenny..." He paused, leaving the inference hanging like a raised guillotine blade.

"I'm sorry, dear...ah...I'm not sure what you're saying..." Sophia stammered. She seemed disoriented; Traveler softened his tone. "I would never allow you to face formal charges," he said, knowing he had no such authority.

Sophia started to babble about the general nature of the case, and her relationship with Jaffee. She discussed in the haziest terms how this could not possibly involve her in felony or murder, and tried to divert the discussion away from the stamps themselves. "You know that I had great affection for my friend. I would never have killed him."

"Sophia, I know you are not a murderer, but there's the problem of alleged theft, and its connection to Jaffee's death. For my own sake, I need to know what happened."

Momentarily more composed, Sophia responded with defiance. "Any part which I may have played in this case was…" She searched for the right word "…incidental."

Then she began earnestly pouring out the whole story, interrupting to berate herself. The full disclosure of a penitent's contrition.

Jaffee, turning to her for advice, had told her about the second sheet of Inverted Jennies. He said he was worried that, in his excitement, he might have inadvertently mentioned his discovery of the Jennies to Princess, as well as Malika; perhaps even a few others; he couldn't recall exactly. Jaffee told Sophia that he had subsequently put the sheet of stamps behind the photograph in his apartment; he *was* sure, at least, that no one else knew their hiding place.

After the bombing, Sophia said, she had taken the next flight back from Europe, rushed to Jaffee's apartment, and retrieved the stamps. She had torn up the apartment to make it look like a burglary, and returned to Europe.

She had found herself immediately confused, distressed, contrite, she said. Unsure what to do with the stamps, in a panic she had called the Philatelic Society's director, and then made the clumsy effort to sell the Jennies in London.

At the same time, Malika thought that she might have seen

Sophia, or someone looking very much like her, leave Jaffee's apartment the night of the faked burglary. Intuition told her to confront Sophia and threaten blackmail. The ultimate outcome was the two agreeing to cooperate in the stamps' disposal.

"But why—why did you steal the stamps?" Traveler cried, despite her attempted explanation. In a deep part of himself, he felt his sense of right and wrong had been violated, that he had been wounded to the quick. "How could you have done this to me?" he shouted.

"Done this to you? To *you*?" she sobbed. "Darling I did this for *us*. Yes, I took the stamps on an insane impulse. I am an imperfect creature. After the London fiasco, Malika and I had determined to abandon any further attempts to sell the Jennies, and turn them over to U.S. authorities. But then I met you..." She hesitated before continuing. "I am not blaming you. I do not see you as responsible in any way.

"Malika then consented to help me contact the ambassador. My only thought was to assure the safety of your and my future together. I had lost that safety before, when my father died. I suddenly saw these stamps as a way for us to be safeguarded and secure forever. I know Joshua would have wanted me to have them. I know—I know—"

# CHAPTER TWENTY-SEVEN

**After Sophia's** tearful admission, Traveler spent several anguished days in deliberation. He decided to speak again with Malika, but with a very different agenda. He had two police officers bring her to the FBI's Hoover building, and upon her arrival he escorted her to the soundproof room in which he had interviewed the Philatelic Society director.

Malika dropped her compact frame into the chair with a thud, the reverberations quickly absorbed by the soundproof walls, and refused Traveler's offer of a beverage.

"You and I have had obvious disagreements in the past," Traveler began evenly; he wanted this to go well. "As a consequence of history and temperament, we do not share similar views of the world, but I believe our objectives are no longer in conflict." He paused to let this suspect notion take hold. "I think you must acknowledge, if not to me, at least to yourself, that circumstances have put you in a difficult position."

"Allah will provide," she replied tersely.

"Yes, I understand and respect that. I understand the importance to you of doing Allah's work. That is part of what I meant by saying we shared a common objective."

She glared at him, but her eyes, like two charcoal orbs

burning with an inner fire, widened involuntarily, betraying a hint of curiosity. "So, you're saying that you and I are now on the same side?" she asked sarcastically.

"Yes and no. I'm not trying to insult you. Regardless of what you may believe, I have too much respect for you for that." He paused, waiting for, hoping for the sincerity of his words to be accepted. Then: "Let me now reiterate the evidence, and I ask that you please hear me out, so that we might better consider the arguments as they will be presented to the jury.

"The government's lawyers will lay out a long list of charges against you. They will ridicule your statement that you were paid to deliver the stamps to the ambassador. This will be described as an insult to common sense and the jury's gullibility. They will cite your father's affiliation with Hezbollah, and his endorsement of the Iranian Shiite theocracy. Your lawyer will protest the circumstantial and misleading nature of all such evidence, but," and Traveler emphasized his next words, "its collective weight will be heavy. The government's arguments will be very, very compelling." Traveler deliberately referred to "the government" as if it were a third party, distancing himself from Malika's adversaries.

"You must also consider the mood of the American public, which will be reflected in the jury. They will be harboring ethnic and religious apprehension that has been revived and amplified by our current administration, as you well know.

Perhaps even more importantly, there is incredible intensity of a more generalized, free-floating anger, eager to find any possible outlet. You will be a target for such anger."

Traveler tried to speak as plainly as he could without provoking her. "This trial will be a witch hunt. The government will seek to exact retribution, and the jury will not have the will to resist." He stopped, considering his next words carefully. "And try to believe me when I say I have no reason to want you to be the object of that retribution." With that, saying all he could to lay the groundwork, he concluded his remarks.

Malika lowered her head and sat quietly, thinking long and hard about what she had heard.

"Yes, I cannot deny that the evidence and the circumstances surrounding this trial do not bode well for me. I expect that I will be found guilty of murder.

"But my personal destiny is unimportant. I live only to serve as an instrument for Allah." She looked toward the ceiling with luminescent eyes, and mouthed something inaudible. "I will never implicate anyone else in this matter. Whatever the political reasons, the government will have its scapegoat, but no one else will be, to borrow from your religion, crucified alongside me."

Traveler seized the opportunity to make his next move. Lowering his voice, he brought his face closer to hers. "The government believes, correctly in my opinion, that its influence with the public is waning rapidly. It wants to shift attention

away from the many domestic problems it is failing to rem-
edy, and spotlight an imaginary enemy, arguing that it alone
is tough enough to struggle with such an adversary. It's a strategy that has worked before."

Though Traveler was barely aware of it, the word "struggle"
described his own plight, as he was falling more deeply in love
with Sophia. He was struggling to fit an altered set of values,
a newly principled geography, onto his Christian moral map.

Traveler now made an irrevocable commitment to saving
the person who had become most important to him.

"The prosecution has evidence," he lied, "that a fanatical
Muslim ideology has infiltrated the Washington police force,
that someone affiliated with a radical group has secured
a position of dangerous influence. The authorities have
finally identified that individual, and your testimony would
confirm it."

"And who might that individual be?" asked Malika, with
studied indifference.

"That individual is Detective Moab.

"The decision you make need not be revealed until you
appear at the trial," Traveler continued quickly. "I can tell you,
and I will have this put in writing for you and your attorney
to review, that if you choose to help identify Detective Moab
as the mastermind of the Lincoln Memorial murder, you will
receive full immunity. All I want you to do is to consider what
I have told you.

"Finally," Traveler said, "and I need not go into the specifics of my involvement, your co-conspirator has identified herself to me." He took another devious route, shown nowhere on his former God-centered cartography. "If you choose to pursue the course I have outlined, the two of you will be equally rewarded from a sale of the Jennies. I can—and you must believe this—guarantee you a buyer and an attractive price."

Malika replied, "Very well. I understand the proposal. Get my attorney the necessary legal papers guaranteeing immunity."

❖

Traveler, the FBI, D.C. police, and the government's legal team held their final preparatory meeting before the trial. Traveler spoke first.

"The Hassan daughter is an obvious candidate for prosecution. She harbors anti-Semitic feelings, had knowledge of the Inverted Jenny stamps and, likely with the help of a co-conspirator, stole them to fund terrorist activities. The bomb was built at the Orpheum theatre, and the theatre was destroyed to cover up evidence." Traveler was doing everything he could to shield Sophia—and to do so had convinced himself that what he was saying essentially conformed with the truth. "It's a very strong case."

At this point, Traveler planted a seed of the idea he had related to Malika. "I also suspect there will be emerging evidence that Malika's associate may very well be someone within the D.C. police force itself."

This obviously caused a stir, but before such speculation could be pursued further, Detective Moab responded with, "What a lot of poppycock." He had been agitated since the beginning of the briefing, twisting and turning in his chair.

"How can you be so ignorant?" he rebuked Traveler. "How do we know that a second sheet of Inverted Jennies even existed? And if it did, that Malika Hassan didn't destroy a copy rather than the real thing? How do we know that a theft of any kind happened?

"There are so many—too many—open questions."

"Obviously, Detective," Traveler replied calmly, "we have no proof that a second set of Jennies ever survived, that the victim Jaffee found them, or that they still might be in someone's possession. That's conjecture, however, that doesn't preclude a murder conviction."

# CHAPTER TWENTY-EIGHT

**The federal courthouse** was just north of Pennsylvania Avenue, a few blocks from the central post office. Two days after the briefing, as the Lincoln Memorial trial opened, the courthouse inevitably turned into a three-ring circus. Demonstrators for and against the accused were out in force, milling about, waving banners, and shouting slogans.

The courtroom was packed. The judge had ostensibly been selected by the usual procedures, free of bias. In fact, this case was far too important to leave anything to chance. The choice had been carefully orchestrated behind the scenes—and the presiding judge was politically ambitious and eager to please his superiors.

Nor did those individuals screened to be the jury pool represent a population of the Hassan daughter's "peers," as there was a preponderance of evangelical Christians and not a single non-Caucasian member—no small feat in a country where the majority of the population had become "persons of color."

The judge went through the formalities, and Malika pleaded not guilty. Then the prosecution called its first witness—none other than Daiyu, the lady of the evening whom Traveler and Savant had met in New York. The authorities had coached her to appear as a prosecution witness, overcoming her reluctance with enough cash to fund years at the race track.

"Ms. Daiyu, you knew the murder victim, Mr. Jaffee, decades ago in New York City. Is that correct?" the prosecutor began.

"Yes, we were friends."

"Would you please elaborate?"

"We shared interests in a lot of things, horse racing among them. My father often took me to the track as I was growing up."

"And what did Mr. Jaffee so enjoy about horse racing?"

"It seemed to tap into something deeply rooted in him. He related it to what he called 'freedom from fear.' " Daiyu was following her script nicely.

"Freedom from fear?" the prosecutor repeated.

"Fear was something we both battled, I guess. Mine was an interracial family. My father had been raised Muslim in Indonesia. My mother, of Asian descent, came from a culture that has been subjected to periodic discrimination in this country. The incarceration of Japanese-Americans during World War II, for example."

The prosecutor followed with a planned, "And this kind of fear, wouldn't you agree, leads to anger, which invites—" Here he vehemently raised his voice. "—violence."

"Objection." Malika's attorney spoke for the first time.

"Sustained."

"And you were raised in the Islamic religion. Is that not true?" continued the district attorney.

"As I said, my father's faith."

"Then you know its history of violence. Of avenging itself against—"

The judge had heard enough. He did not want to risk a mistrial. "Where are you going with this, counsel? This is not a religious debate. Enough of the rhetoric."

"Certainly, your honor." Then, immediately violating the judge's admonition, "Of course Mr. Jaffee was afraid. Who wouldn't be, surrounded by alien religious persecution—"

Traveler watched from the gallery. The prosecutor had not used Daiyu's association with Jaffee's earlier version of himself to produce any evidence against Malika. Daiyu had simply been a Trojan horse for bombastic rabble rousing. The questions and contentions were nonsensical, and the distortions extreme—but not without effect, Traveler knew.

"Save the grandstanding for your summation speech, counselor," the judge interjected. "I won't warn you again."

"Yes, your honor. The prosecution has no more questions for this witness."

Next Traveler took the stand. The prosecutor first asked him to describe the scene of the explosion, which he used as a pretext to exhort the jury to appreciate the malevolent extent of the carnage. Traveler then lead the jury through each phase of the investigation, and offered his opinion that the case had all the earmarks of a hate crime, and that everything the police and FBI had uncovered about Jaffee's activities pointed to enemies within the Islamic community. He informed the jury of Malika's background, her family's history in Lebanon, and her father's radical Shiite connections. He also recounted how Jaffee had discovered and hidden a second sheet of priceless Inverted Jennies, and lastly outlined the turning point in the investigation: the report of an attempted high-profile stamp transaction in London that had prompted the sting operation leading to Malika's arrest.

Before he stepped down from the witness stand, however, to the district attorney's surprise, he added, "And it was my impression, though I cannot prove it, that Malika Hassan may have had help from someone within our city's own criminal justice system."

The defense attorney had repeatedly jumped to his feet, shouting "Hearsay!" as incriminating evidence against his client mounted. But the cumulative weight, as Traveler had suggested, was considerable, and after a few hours, the prosecution was content to rest.

"In that case, ladies and gentlemen," the judge declared, "we will reconvene next Tuesday. Court is adjourned."

# CHAPTER TWENTY-NINE

**When the trial** reconvened, the defense called its first witness: Princess, Joshua Jaffee's post office colleague, who had so narrowly missed being killed herself. The intent was to establish that persons other than his client might have had motive for the murder.

Unlike everyone else in the courtroom, Princess, true to form, appeared dressed more as if she were attending a gala party than appearing as a witness in a court of law.

She sashayed up to the stand in a flowing caftan splashed with a colorful, swirling abstract pattern. She had not stinted on makeup, either, with a rainbow of eye shadow tints, liberally applied mascara and fire-engine-red lipstick. Reading glasses with neon-green frames hung from her neck on a gaudily beaded string.

The defense attorney, ignoring her bizarre outfit, began his questioning with a businesslike, "How well did you know the deceased?"

"We worked together at the post office for about ten years or so."

"That's a fairly long time. Certainly you must have learned quite a bit about his personal interests and habits."

"Is that a statement or question?" she asked, drawing a low ripple of laughter from the packed courtroom. The judge lightly tapped his gavel for order.

"A question."

"Okay, yes, ten years is a relatively long time. Post office time would double that. We joke that post office time goes by twice as slowly as regular time."

"Did you ever suspect that Mr. Jaffee had enemies angry enough to kill him?"

"I'm not aware that he had any personal enemies." So far, Princess wasn't giving the defense attorney much help.

"What about his political activities? He must have confided that he felt threatened by any number of people reacting to his radical religious opinions?"

"Yes, as timid as he appeared, it was amazing how he could periodically transform himself into an outraged zealot. Almost Jekyll and Hyde."

"You must have known about the Inverted Jenny stamps."

Princess was taken aback by the bold assertion. The defense attorney moved towards her with seemingly predatory intent. "Your answer," he demanded.

"Well...I...maybe I did."

"Is that a yes?"

Princess, always eager to be the center of attention, now thought she spotted an opportunity to assume a starring role in the proceedings—to be seen as someone of consequence, someone who possessed singularly newsworthy insight into the case. She threw all caution aside.

"Why, of course I knew about the stamps. No one was closer to Joshua than I was. No one knew more about him than I did." She looked around the courtroom in triumph.

"So it would have been natural for you to conspire with someone to sell the Inverted Jennies?"

Her look of triumph vanished, as she perceived the difficult position she might have so impulsively put herself in. "No. Wait a minute. Yes, I looked for the stamps in his apartment, after his terrible death, but the place had already been torn apart—"

Now struck by the full extent of her self-induced predicament, she burst into tears. "Oh my God, I could never have killed him—never, never. I loved him," she blurted. Like attacking a set of worry beads, her fingers feverishly worked over the string attached to her reading glasses.

"No more questions," said the defense. Princess left the witness stand, sniffling.

Throughout the colloquy between lawyer and witness, the prosecution had repeatedly raised objections, but the defense attorney successfully had them dismissed, arguing that he was only helping the jury understand that more than one individual existed as a possible suspect—thus raising clear "reasonable doubt" regarding his client's guilt.

The director of the Washington Philatelic Society was the

next defense witness. There could not have been a more reluctant participant, as he worried that he would not be able to
carry out Traveler's instructions. In fact, the defense had called
him merely with the prospect of generating additional pre-
sumptions of reasonable doubt.

"You have played a role in this investigation because of your
expertise in stamp collecting, correct?" the attorney began.

"Yes," the director replied.

"What was your introduction to the case?"

"Washington police brought to me for evaluation the stamp
collection found in Mr. Jaffee's apartment."

"And what was the nature of your assessment?"

"As I told Detective Moab, what I found most interesting was
the collection's thematic identity."

"Please explain." The director gave the jury an abbrevi-
ated version of his conversation with Moab. "Is there anything
else you could share with us that might be relevant to this
investigation?"

The attorney was trying to snag some shred of narrative,
any shred that might divert suspicion from his client.

"Well, perhaps..." the director started, then broke off,
hesitating.

"Go on," the attorney urged.

The director took a deep breath. With Traveler's directions
foremost in his mind, he plunged ahead. "It was my observation that Detective Moab was unusually knowledgeable about

stamps, and that he was not at all surprised by Mr. Jaffee's fascination with the airmails. I found this quite unexpected."

The attorney turned away from the witness and faced the jury. "I see. It would make one wonder, wouldn't it, as to why the detective would have such knowledge. I'm sure this will prove valuable as we explore other possible motives and other possible suspects."

"Objection, your honor."

"I have no further questions for the witness," the defense attorney said. Returning to his seat, he waited for the next witness to be called—his client.

❖

That morning, before court began, Malika's lawyer made one last attempt at advising her not to testify. He argued that he had decisively undermined the prosecution's case, and that depending on any assurance of immunity was unacceptably fraught with risk. But Malika had insisted on, as she put it, "her day in court."

"The defense calls Ms. Hassan." Malika rose, and with head held high, marched to the front of the courtroom.

"Do you swear to tell the truth, the whole truth, and nothing but the truth, so help you God?"

"As Allah would have it." She had insisted that she be sworn in placing her hand on a copy of the Quran. "Yes." She stated her name and address for the record.

"The prosecution has alleged that your brother was involved in the Lincoln Memorial incident, and that his place of business, the Orpheum theatre, was used for constructing the bomb, and was later burned to destroy evidence. Moreover, it has been suggested he was killed in the process."

"Objection. Is there a question, your honor?"

"Sustained."

"Let me rephrase, then. What can you tell us about any of your brother's activities that might have a bearing on this case?"

"My brother is a charitable, innocent man, and any form of brutality is beyond his comprehension, much less his capability. I use the present tense in speaking of him, because he is very much alive and is living with friends in Beirut."

At this revelation, the courtroom began buzzing. Malika's contention ran counter to all official accounts about her brother. The judge rapped his gavel for order, and the room fell silent as Malika's attorney quickly moved to the line of questioning that Traveler had eagerly and anxiously awaited.

"You have stated previously that you were given money anonymously to deliver stamps to the African ambassador, and that while doing so you were engaged in a phone conversation of an ordinary business nature. Would you now like to expand on that explanation?"

"I have always tried to remain steadfast to the cause of Allah, and loyal to fellow believers. Perhaps I have been too ardent in my loyalties."

"Go on."

"I do not approve of violence, nor have I engaged in any violent act. I may be guilty of naively accepting money to act out the drama that took place at the African embassy, but I trusted the individual who had sent me on the errand. The individual who sent me to the African ambassador and with whom I was conversing on the cell phone..." Malika paused. The air seemed to have been sucked out of the courtroom, as if everyone in it had simultaneously drawn in a breath, holding it as they waited for her answer.

"...was Detective Moab of the Washington police force."

The room erupted in pandemonium, as Moab was identified in the courtroom. The judge attempted with futility to call the courtroom to order, but was compelled to declare a recess, and the media representatives frantically rushed out to inform their news agencies of the startling trial development.

As an atmosphere of the surreal set in, Moab offered no resistance as two police officers quickly flanked him, placed his hands behind his back and cuffed him. Indeed, he felt a queer sense of the inevitable, but even as the officers led him away, silently vowed to fight the forces that had always conspired against him.

## CHAPTER THIRTY

**Malika was still** being held in custody, of course, though the prosecution had agreed to a mistrial, preferring to pursue a case against Moab. Within days of his arrest, Moab's court-appointed lawyer—Moab declaring himself insolvent—sat him down for a candid talk.

It was widely known that Moab's mental state was in question; thus his attorney advised him that pleading insanity would be his most effective defense.

Moab flatly refused, insulted by the suggestion. The attorney had barely finished offering his advice when Moab launched into a diatribe against "the system," a nameless, ill-defined "they" who had been plotting against him all these years.

"They have never let me get ahead, standing in my way, cheating me at every turn. Who wouldn't be vengeful? I'm entitled. I'm justified."

Each passing moment, as Moab worked himself into more of a lather, only further convinced his attorney that "insanity" was the correct, believable plea. He could only beg, again and again, "Please. Just consider it."

Moab sat in jail over the next week or so; his trial had been expedited because of the notoriety of the case. His lawyer continued to implore him to see that an insanity plea was his best chance to avoid life in prison, given the evidence—real, circumstantial or fictitious—that the government would parade before a jury. Just as it had done in Malika's trial.

Yet, Moab remained steadfast. He believed that he was not only sane, but had a more accurate comprehension of how the world worked than most.

He insisted not only on testifying, but on being questioned by the government prosecutor himself. Although he was being tried as the sole perpetrator of the Lincoln Memorial murder, he believed—no, he knew—his testimony would explain everything, and he would be vindicated.

The government felt its strategy only required some minor "redefinitions," a slight reframing of the case. An "enemy of the people," though perhaps no longer solely Islamic jihadists, could still be exploited for political gain. Moab, after all, was half-Arab, long affiliated with the Muslim community, and could be portrayed as simply another version of deadly fanatic.

Moab's trial was in many ways a repeat of Malika's—it proceeded with much of the same evidence, and many of the same allegations. The critical testimony, obviously, would come from Moab himself, and the prosecutor, a white, middle-aged man with a crew cut, now rose and approached the stand where Moab sat, stone-faced.

"Detective," the prosecutor began, "you are a member of the Washington police department, is that correct?"

"Yes, a police officer for more than twenty years."

"And what motivated you to pursue this line of work?"

"I was raised in a family where there were many difficulties. My father was Jewish, my mother an Islamic Arab. I think a common ambition held them together."

"What common ambition was that, Detective?"

"Each of them was a displaced person. Each of them was determined to succeed. In America, they supported one another in this quest."

"Was this related to the family 'difficulties' you mentioned?"

"The bond between my parents was the desire to make good. The end was the same, but they differed on the means."

"How so?"

"They both loved American democracy, but my father encouraged me to be aggressive, hard working, and single-minded."

"Your mother?"

"She would simply say to me, 'Allah will provide.'"

"What influence did these dissenting views have on you?"

"It ultimately strengthened my determination to help protect our great democracy." Moab's counsel had done his best to prepare him for this line of questioning, and the detective was following his advice, at least so far.

"Please explain."

"I wanted to use police work to make democracy successful for all of us, to make the system more fair and just. I had very noble ambitions."

"And has your work helped you realize those ambitions, Detective?"

"Most certainly. It was my idea to establish an antiterrorism unit within Washington's police force. I recognized the tensions that might very well arise and escalate between those faithful to different religions. After all, I had lived with them myself."

"And is it true that you spent a great deal of time on this task force reaching out to the Islamic community?"

"Yes, absolutely. It was imperative that we establish lines of communication with all members of the community."

The prosecutor took a few steps back from the witness and turned to the jury; then, still facing the jury, asked Moab, "You have heard the allegations made against you, Detective. How do you respond?"

"The evidence against me is hearsay. These allegations are false. I am innocent of the charges that have been brought against me," said Moab, rising slightly from his chair. The prosecution's objective was to start pushing him onto a psychological tightrope.

"Detective, as an expert in the field of investigative police work, have you arrived at your own theory about the motive for the Lincoln Memorial crime?"

"Yes, I have."

The jury leaned forward as one.

"No one knows the conditions for terrorism in this city better than I, and from the very beginning I felt that alleging 'Islamic jihad' as the motive was too simplistic, not credible. It severely constricted our investigation."

"And what, in your opinion, was the reason for such an excessive limiting of investigative focus?"

"My sense was that political pressures were being brought to bear by the system."

Moab's voice trembled ever so slightly. The prosecutor betrayed the merest hint of a knowing smile: the genie had poked its head out of the bottle.

"The system isn't always right. In fact, the system is more often than not rigged to prevent fairness and justice," Moab declared forcefully. A muscle in his cheek started to twitch. The prosecutor carefully but inexorably pushed him further onto the tightrope.

"The woman who is known as Princess has suggested that the two of you were romantically involved, and that you likely knew about Mr. Jaffee's Inverted Jenny stamps."

"Not true. We are acquainted. But, as I'm sure everyone has observed," he said disdainfully, "she is prone to hysteria."

"So you're suggesting—"

"I'm suggesting that I had no reason to be jealous of Joshua Jaffee, certainly with any intent of committing murder."

"There was no, how should I put this, love triangle?"

Moab replied scornfully, "The idea is absurd. You've seen her. How could anyone imagine that two men, no matter how desperate, would seriously fight over her?" The comment did not play well with two middle-aged, heavyset female jurors, who could be seen shaking their heads in disgust.

"Detective, Ms. Hassan has previously testified that you were her accomplice in the attempted sale of the Inverted Jennies. Your answer?"

"I am at a complete loss as to why she would make such an accusation. I knew about the sting operation, and it would have been foolish to conspire with her under the circumstances." Aware of his previous slips in emotional equilibrium, Moab was trying to steady himself.

The prosecution headed in another direction.

"Let's return, for a moment, to your objections to an Islamic hate crime motive—"

Moab broke in, "Fear-mongering is an old ruse the system often uses," picking up on his earlier thought. "It's a way to create enemies to rally against." He sounded pleased with what he viewed as his savvy understanding of political skullduggery.

"I see. Moving on, Detective. As head of Washington's anti-terrorism unit, you gained the trust of the Islamic community as a conciliatory figure, correct?"

"I would hope so."

The prosecutor returned to his chair, picked up a folder,

paged through its contents for several moments, then said, "Washington police records show that authorities have repeatedly been unable to make arrests in terrorism cases due to what your fellow police officers have described as 'insider infiltration.' What's your view?" Such records, of course, were nonexistent.

"If there ever have been such allegations, they've never been proven."

The prosecutor veered in another direction again, seeking to further destabilize Moab.

"It has also been reported that you have demolitions experience. Is that correct?"

"Early in my career I had occasion to receive training in explosives, but many people know how to construct the kind of explosive used at the Lincoln Memorial. It was not that sophisticated."

"It has been asserted that the device used to destroy the Inverted Jennies at the ambassador's office was more sophisticated. Is that accurate?"

"Perhaps. I'd have to review the details again to say for sure."

The prosecutor continued attempting to force a fall to earth for the unsteady man on the wobbling tightrope by brandishing a new interrogative provocation.

"The director of the Philatelic Society has testified that in the conversation the two of you had, you showed no surprise about Mr. Jaffee's valuable stamp collection. He had the distinct impression that you knew a great deal about the victim and his airmail stamps."

"The director is free to have formed any impression he likes. That doesn't change the fact that I'm telling the truth," said Moab, his voice rising. "I did not steal any Inverted Jennies and I did not kill anyone."

The detective's face had taken on a deepening shade of red as the questioning proceeded. Moab was losing his balance, teetering on the edge of volcanic rage.

"I empathized with Jaffee, after all," Moab said. His breath started coming in harsh rasps. "We both knew what it was like to live with warring impulses. It's all a rigged game, with the powerful trapping the powerless. A large monster of lobbyists, fundraisers, ideological groups," he sputtered. "The whole process of governing in this country, the greedy, self-preoccupied ruling class—"

The rant was taking on a life of its own; Moab's attorney sunk his head into his hands. Through it all the judge repeatedly pounded his gavel, to little effect. Moab, flecks of foam gathering at the corners of his mouth, spouted a stream of epithets— "brain-dead religious right-wing evangelical fanatics—"

The sound of the gavel hitting the desk and the rising roar from the crowd in the courtroom, as if in a circus tent, provided the backdrop as Moab, having completely lost his footing, fell away from any semblance of innocence.

"Yes. Raise the jihad sword, by God—"

Moab had confirmed the advisability of an insanity plea.

❖

Moab's attorney decided not to subject his client to further court-room trauma, preferring to move immediately to summation speeches. The next day the jury heard closing arguments.

"Ladies and gentlemen of the jury," the defense counsel began, "these proceedings have made liberal use of distortion, innuendo, and circumstantial evidence. You've been subjected to charges and countercharges. And certainly my client's behavior yesterday has not helped his cause.

"Yes, he is a man who feels profoundly victimized. Yes, his way of seeing the world may be at the outer fringes of what many of us might describe as 'normal.' And when he feels under stress, his sense of righteous indignation is sometimes expressed in an unseemly fashion. This I apologize for, and, I assure you, he deeply regrets.

"My client has worked painfully to secure a small portion of the American dream. He has served the Washington police department faithfully and admirably, committed to keeping us safe in this increasingly dangerous world. We owe him a sincere debt of gratitude.

"His only crime, if you were to call it that, has been to become enmeshed in a web of damning circumstances. There is not a shred of proof that he was involved in the Lincoln Memorial bombing, no hard evidence whatsoever.

"I would ask you to take seriously my client's contention that, from the outset, a group of powerful people, for political and social reasons, have desired a certain outcome from this investigation. All of us have grown weary of 'conspiracy theories,' but we live in fearful times, in which there is often political gain from demonizing what makes us afraid.

"When I began representing him, I did not know my client well, but I do now. Let me assure you that he is not, nor has ever been, a threat to any of us.

"Religious beliefs, and what we might do to defend those beliefs, have been at the heart of this trial. For those of you of the Christian faith, recall that Christ was used as a sacrificial lamb by the religious and political authorities of his day, as a warning to others not to challenge prevailing orthodoxy. I ask you to consider Detective Moab as someone who has fallen victim to similar events and conditions."

With that, the defense attorney took his seat. By most accounts, it had been an effective presentation. The prosecutor now rose from his chair, and, fastening the single button on his jacket, approached the jury.

"The defense attorney's words are, I'm sure, heartfelt. I'm sure that he sincerely believes in the innocence of his client.

"However, your responsibility, ladies and gentlemen of the jury, has been made fairly simple by the laws of our land. You

are being asked to judge if the accused is guilty of the lethal
mayhem committed at the Lincoln Memorial 'beyond any
reasonable doubt.'

"Let us reflect on that standard of judgment. The evidence
supporting the guilt of the accused is staggering. Like the
defense attorney, I will inject a personal observation. Never,
in my many years of prosecuting cases, have I come across a
situation where so many facts and individuals point in the same
direction. They all point to Detective Moab as the perpetrator
of this heinous deed.

"Let me summarize the evidence for you once again. The
accused, as we have witnessed, and as his own counsel admits,
is a man consumed by hatred. He sees enemies everywhere,
what he calls the Establishment, the system, evangelical
Christian fanatics, white Anglo-Saxon elitists, power-hungry
and unscrupulous political groups—the list goes on and on.

"Through this rage, he has come to identify with another
aggregation of disaffected souls, Islamic fanatics. He has
welded his rage to theirs. He found Mr. Jaffee's religious protests maddening.

"Ms. Hassan, although valuing the empathy Detective Moab
has shown for the Islamic community, and Princess, the woman
who loves him—both have supported the allegation that he,
and he alone, committed the Lincoln Memorial atrocity.

"Not only did he have temperamental motivation to com-
mit this crime, he also had financial motive. Although the

accused has only been charged with murder, he might also have been charged with grand larceny. The stamps in question, the Inverted Jennies, were worth a fortune, and would likely have brought the affluence, respect, and recognition he believed he deserved. He would finally have achieved what both he and his parents before him had always so distressfully sought—a fulfillment of the American dream.

"Finally, let me make it absolutely clear that this is not a vendetta on the part of some conspiratorial group, particularly one composed of government officials. Even suggesting such a thing, I would submit, is profoundly offensive and insults us all. The suggestion that those who have devoted their lives to preserving our laws—that they are corrupt hypocrites—is beyond contempt.

"Common sense, ladies and gentlemen. All that I ask, that your countrymen ask, and that the Constitution asks, is that you apply to your deliberations your common sense, and any reasonably accepted notion of justice—and render a verdict of guilty."

The prosecutor returned to his seat. Traveler sat in the audience imagining the man crossing the courtroom, cloaked in an American flag.

# CHAPTER THIRTY-ONE

**The jury began** its deliberations. The group of seven women and five men had listened to conflicting voices and opinions about the Lincoln Memorial tragedy, and the apparent theft of priceless airmail stamps. To be sure, there were factual underpinnings to the case: explosive devices, letters, e-mails, personal histories of the drama's major characters, substantiated conversations and actions—but no indisputable proof to tilt the scales of justice decisively in one direction or the other.

Within this context, the foreman, an unassuming man who had recently moved to Washington to care for his elderly mother, opened the proceedings.

"Before we begin discussing the case, I'd suggest we take a secret straw vote to get a general idea of where we're at. Any objections?"

With all in agreement, writing materials were passed throughout the room, and each person wrote "guilty" or "innocent" on a slip of paper. The ballots were passed back to the foreman, counted, and announced.

"We have eight 'guilty' and four 'innocent' votes," the foreman said. "Okay, let's hear reasons for either verdict."

The twelve men and women began trading perspectives. Clearly, most had been mightily swayed by Moab's display of angst.

"He seems like such a terrible man, un-American, really," one woman complained.

"He's deranged. Capable of anything," said another.

Arguments for guilt or innocence were traded back and forth. As the afternoon dragged on and it became clear no consensus was forming, the jury retired for the day.

The next morning, the foreman opened the session by walking to the blackboard; he wrote "guilty" to the left and "innocent" to the right.

"Let's start this morning by making a list of reasons to vote either way. I'll write them down." He appeared somewhat experienced at resolving conflict; he was a retired dentist, and had likely learned over the years how to soothe angry patients.

He was also a dutiful son, now burdened with the expensive care of his ailing mother; the cost was reaching a level beyond his ability to pay. If this fact were known to no one else, it could never remain hidden from one individual, who knew, or could find out, anything about anyone.

That individual was, of course, the Chairman, who had arranged for the foreman to be generously compensated in return for guiding the jury to a guilty verdict.

"Under 'guilty' put 'violent nature,'" said one juror.

"Add 'sides with Islamic fanatics,'" said another.

"Put 'no hard evidence' in the 'innocent' column."

The process continued throughout most of the morning. The foreman, who repeatedly returned to notations on the blackboard, methodically changed and clarified language.

By mid-afternoon, the group seemed ready to take a second straw vote. This time the result was ten "guilty" and two "innocent."

❖

At the ensuing session, the foreman made no effort to quell the emotional pot that was simmering. Ten jurors began to sharply confront the two members not yet prepared to find Moab guilty. "What's your hang-up?" one shouted.

The two holdouts were women, one in her thirties, a stay-at-home mother of three, the other a sixty-two-year-old schoolteacher. They sat next to one another near the end of the conference room table. Although separated by nearly thirty years, their speech, dress, and demeanor stereotyped them as suburban middle class. Throughout the discussions, although in an obvious minority, they had reinforced one another's viewpoint. The older woman was the first to respond to her fellow juror's challenge.

"What's my hang-up? Well, there's that little thing called 'reasonable doubt.' Too many reasons to doubt his guilt. I believe Mr. Jaffee was murdered over the stamps. Five hundred million dollars is more than enough money to kill for—"

"If such a theft ever occurred," came the disgusted reply.

"But Jaffee's apartment was turned upside down," said the woman.

The jurors continued to volley back and forth as the hours ticked by. The younger woman who had voted for acquittal was clearly starting to succumb to the collective harassment. Seeing another opening, the foreman abandoned any pretense of neutral mediator, yelling, "Let's take another vote, and this time make it unanimous!"

Again they passed around pens and paper; again the makeshift ballots were counted: eleven "guilty" and one "innocent." The older woman, now the lone dissenter, stubbornly fought on until day's end.

On the fourth day, eleven jurors returned ready to wear down the single holdout.

Before she even had a chance to speak, one of the jurors jumped up and started shouting at her. "I don't understand you," the man said, shaking his finger at her in barely concealed fury. "You're intelligent, maybe too intelligent. Don't over think this.

"Common sense dictates we find the accused guilty. We can sit and debate the pros and cons forever, but our heads and hearts are telling us what to do. Submitting a guilty verdict, for a man so conflicted and capable of committing any act, no matter how horrible, is the only decision that makes common sense. We need to remove him from our midst."

He had summarized the fatigue-fueled frustration of his ten fellow jurors. How could she persist in her ridiculous over-protection of the rights of the individual at the expense of the common good?

The teacher, however, was no longer in any mood to continue opposing the majority view. Overnight, the situation had changed.

It had been conveyed to her, in no uncertain terms, that continuing to oppose the majority position would result in dire consequences for her family.

That afternoon, the jury filed back into the courtroom. The foreman of the jury stood, and read the verdict: "We find the accused guilty of murder in the first degree."

# CHAPTER THIRTY-TWO

**Traveler had paradoxical feelings** about the verdict. He had protected Sophia, but it had become indisputable that the current political regime—part of what Moab had characterized as the Establishment—was indeed badly compromised.

Jesus had promised that "the meek shall inherit the earth." It was a promise, Traveler now sensed, that would never be brought to fruition.

As he left the courtroom, his cane slipped out from under him and he stumbled slightly. As he righted himself, Traveler accepted the undeniability that his born-again faith would never again provide the stability to his life that it once had.

❖

The president of the United States was sitting at his laptop in an antechamber off the Oval Office when he heard the news of the verdict. He smiled, filled with satisfaction, walked into the Oval Office, and made a call to a remote island off the coast of South America.

"Yes," the Chairman agreed, "this is truly a day you will remember." The president was unaware of the statement's irony.

# CHAPTER THIRTY-THREE

**Reverend Christian's** attacks on the cocaine trade began early in December, when the holiday season was already in full swing, with advertising starting shortly after Labor Day, in a frantic effort to sell something, anything, to a tapped out American consumer.

Christian's daily broadcasts were from his headquarters in a seaside town in the southeast corner of Virginia.

Everything Christian did was writ large. He had raised—or lowered, depending on your view—to new levels the excessive style of previous renowned proselytizers. He relished his "drug crusade," which drew on all his persuasive talents.

His sermons began by painting a lurid picture of America's ills across a broad canvas—disrespectful children, unwed mothers, casual sex, general moral decay—then gradually narrowed the public's attention to what he called the "core corruptions." Heading that list were illicit drugs, with the most corrupting of all, the devil cocaine.

He had pseudo-documentaries produced that dramatized in the most sensational way the evils of cocaine. The public was immediately tantalized by the first documentary, the story of a virtuous young man who abandons his position as star quarterback on his high school football team, his presidency of the school's student body, and his duties delivering food to the elderly each weekend—as he falls prey to the town's burgeoning drug culture. In other productions, marriages are destroyed and careers ruined—all thanks to the demon cocaine.

Gradually, Reverend Christian's vilifications zeroed in on Colombia's cocaine trafficking network. His followers grew familiar with maps of the country, shown in detail, down to specific drug transport routes, from planting fields to the marketplace.

The Reverend's "personal" drug war was imbued with the same medieval righteousness that had driven Christian knights to make their crusades to the Holy Land. Colombia was Jerusalem, held captive by modern-day heathens, the drug lords.

An increasing number of blogs, editorials, and letters-to-the-editor appeared, lamenting the U.S. cocaine culture. The mainstream media slavishly turned its attention to what was now broadly known as the Cocaine Crusade. Rappers and other avatars of popular music were hired by the Reverend's organization to produce songs denouncing the drug.

It was all coming together. Reverend Christian was on his way to achieving global celebrity status, fame greater than anything he had ever known before.

❖

As Christmas approached, Reverend Christian announced he would be taking his daily broadcasts to the Pacific coast of Colombia. Years earlier, as a part of worldwide outreach efforts, he had established Grace Church, a small missionary outpost in the Valle del Cauca, northeast of Cali, in a coastal town called Buenaventura.

The Pacific fringe of the Valle, humid and mostly jungle, was important to the coca-growing industry. Local narcotics dealers owned hotels, restaurants, supermarkets in the area. Reverend Christian proclaimed that he would enter the "lion's den," to confront the enemy in his lair.

Getting Christian to tiny Buenaventura was a logistics nightmare, involving television equipment, directors, writers, lighting and sound technicians, and a small acting entourage. The town had never seen anything like it.

The Chairman had arranged for the most sophisticated media satellite communications to cover the Reverend's ministry in South America. The programs would reach an even larger audience than those originating from Virginia.

The shift of venue was, of course, all part of the larger plan. The three Cali brothers would spearhead the abduction. They had hand-picked a half-dozen men who would seize the Reverend in mid-broadcast, and take him to a secret location along the Magdalena River in Colombia's northern sector. There, the Medellin cartel would take over.

The first two broadcasts from Buenaventura occurred without incident. The actors recreated Christ's confrontation with the money changers as a theatrical musical, an evangelical opera of sorts. The story had been rewritten with Reverend Christian in the starring role, confronting drug lords in modern-day Colombia. Christian played himself, with the rest of the cast as narco-terrorists. It was all high energy, filled with song, dance, and halleluiahs.

The kidnapping itself was scheduled for the third broadcast, to assure a full complement of media. Several planes had been chartered for bloggers, Internet pundits, and press and television crews, who assumed they were just documenting the ratings-worthy antics of another internationally known public figure.

The sermon topic of the third broadcast was "Christmas as Celebration." The Reverend regaled the thousands outside Grace Church in a joyful celebration not only of the birth of Jesus Christ, but the birth of a new era of everlasting evangelical righteousness. At the conclusion of his sermon, as the Reverend began a thunderously worded prayer, six masked men with automatic weapons suddenly rushed forward.

The local people and media watched, frozen in place; the men ran up to the pulpit, grabbed Reverend Christian, and dragged him from the stage. The crowd, once overcoming its astonishment, descended into wild riot.

❖

Within minutes, the news had been relayed throughout the world: Reverend Christian, leader of the Cocaine Crusade, had apparently been kidnapped. The worst was feared. His world-wide audience stayed glued to their PCs and TVs. Among them were millions of new followers, brought to the fold by his campaign against the merchants of violence and death.

As for the Reverend Christian, he now was comfortably ensconced in the great room of a sumptuous lodge in the Magdalena valley. After the masked men had hustled him into a waiting getaway car, he had been taken to an inconspicuous landing strip just outside the town, and flown by private aircraft to the lodge, an isolated retreat for the top echelon of the Medellin cocaine empire. A fire burned in the large hearth to take the chill out of the late-evening air, and Christian sat before the crackling flames, martini in hand, watching the BBC highlight his presumed abduction.

Within days, a copy of a ransom note from a group calling itself the Colombian Freedom Fighters was leaked to the media. The note talked about U.S. imperialism and the victimization of Colombia's poor farmers. Instead of money, the kidnappers demanded that certain "political prisoners" be released.

The Reverend was enjoying a lavish lunch with his drug-lord "captors" as he listened to the latest news regarding his plight. Unexpectedly, his stomach lurched.

As he had accepted his part in the kidnapping scheme many months ago, he had failed to think beyond receiving the universal attention he anticipated.

Now, as he sat breaking bread with his unsavory companions, it dawned on him that he might be caught in a larger dangerous drama.

He abruptly stood up. "I want to see Sophia," he demanded.

The next morning, Reverend Christian found himself looking out over the verdant forest, sipping strong coffee with Colombia's Catholic cardinal—and the ever reappearing Savant.

The Chairman had decided to send Savant because there was no one else he trusted more, but also because Savant possessed an intimate understanding of Colombia's internal political turmoil; Savant knew that guerrilla fighters, composed of peasants and unemployed urban youth, were engaging in pitched battles against cattlemen and ranchers. The landowners, in turn, continued to expand their own paramilitary forces. Savant had an unusual appreciation for how the cocaine traffickers were in the middle, trying their best to turn events to their advantage.

As an avid ornithologist, Savant also eagerly took advantage of the opportunity for an up-close look at the birdlife indigenous to the middle Magdalena valley: the blue-billed curassow, sooty ant tanager, white mantled barbet, and Antioquia bristle tyrant.

On the veranda, Christian, the cardinal, and Savant enjoyed their coffee as the sun rose. Savant took his binoculars and scanned the horizon, hoping to catch a blue-billed curassow.

"The curassow is usually active during this time of day," he remarked to no one in particular.

The Reverend had been able to keep his composure and remain relatively cordial. Ignoring Savant's inane ornithological observation, he asked, "So tell me, gentlemen, what's the meaning of all this ransom nonsense I'm hearing about?

"The plan outlined to me involved my rather quick release, after which I would report a daring escape, and vow to continue my fight against drug smuggling—sending my popularity and church donations through the roof."

The cardinal responded first. "Reverend Christian, I bring greetings from Ms. Sophia, and she assures me that no harm will come to you. All the wheels are in motion, I believe you would say in your country, to secure your release."

The Medellin cartel hosts, including its *capo,* the handsome man to whom Sophia had been introduced, stepped from the interior of the lodge onto the veranda. The cardinal greeted them warmly. "Buenos días, my good friends. It is so good to see you again. It has been too long."

The cardinal had begun his pastoral work nearby in the town of Yarumal, just north of Medellin, and had gotten to know the cartel's men well during his tenure there.

Reverend Christian sat open-mouthed. He had never trusted Catholics much, but these Medellin guys were criminals, for God's sake. "I...I'm amazed that you know each other," he sputtered.

"Yes, we and the cardinal have championed the cause of our country's common people for many decades now. Brothers-in-arms, you might say."

The cardinal smiled.

"Well, that's just terrific," Christian replied caustically, "but tell me, gentlemen, when, exactly, do I get out of here?"

The cardinal repeated his earlier assurances. "It is only a matter of days now, Reverend Christian. I hope that you have not found our hospitality displeasing?"

The Reverend altered his tone. "No, of course not, but I have important issues to take care of in the United States. The public has a short attention span, so I need to leverage this kidnapping thing as quickly as possible."

Savant's periodic meandering about on the porch, peering through his binoculars, was starting to grate on Christian. He turned to him, and in an irritated voice asked, "What word do you bring from the Chairman's organization?"

Savant put down his binoculars. "Oh, I'm completely familiar with the kidnapping hoax," he replied with a distracted air, "and the Chairman merely asked me to observe the discussions and report back."

"Well, great—great." Christian's ire was on the ascent again. "Here I am with a Papist, drug smugglers, and a nincompoop—" He stopped in mid-sentence, recognizing that he had perhaps once again gone too far. "You'll have to excuse me, gentlemen," he said contritely. "It's just that the inactivity and the news reports have put me on edge."

"We understand, Reverend Christian," the cardinal replied

soothingly. "The strain of such situations often makes one say things that are not intended."

"Yes, exactly. Thank you for understanding." What the cardinal understood was that Christian had meant what he said, but hadn't intended to express what he meant.

The Medellin cartel's leader took up the conversation. "Señor Christian, we have just been speaking directly with the president of Colombia, who guarantees that as soon as possible a statement will be issued announcing that you have been safely transported back to the U.S.

"He will not offer any details other than that the escape necessitated exceptional bravery on your part—and he will subsequently confirm whatever you choose to report about the incident."

# CHAPTER THIRTY-FOUR

**As the Reverend sat** in his resort-cum-prison in Colombia awaiting release, Traveler was also feeling a sense of captivity— to the Lincoln Memorial imbroglio. After the trial concluded, the Chairman had insisted that Traveler help bring to light the "truth" behind the crime. To leave no loose ends, the Chairman wanted to know who *had* killed Joshua Jaffee, after all?

Traveler went back to square one, reviewing physical evidence in the case: the explosive device, everything in Malika Hassan's living quarters, Jaffee's few possessions, the stamp sale and trial documents.

He had arrived at the point where he was scrutinizing the photograph discovered in Jaffee's room, showing him as a youngster holding the hand of an older woman. Successfully prosecuting the case had not necessitated learning more about the relationship between Jaffee and the woman.

As Traveler examined the photo under magnification, he could just barely make out a design on a pin on the woman's uniform. It appeared that it might be an airline logo, which fit with Sophia's understanding that Jaffee's aunt had been an airline stewardess.

Traveler turned to the Internet to see if he could identify the logo. It took a little digging, since airlines had gone through numerous mergers in the ensuing years, but he finally found a match. He called the airline's Washington office, and made an appointment to see the human resources manager.

"You're fortunate, sir, that we still have photos on file of all our employees, going back to the 1930s." The bureaucrat's pride was evident. "Give me a day or so, and we'll provide whatever information we have on this woman."

In two days, he had the name, Hannah Feldman, and last known address, the Chicago YWCA. Traveler was again fortunate that the YWCA also kept excellent records, and Ms. Feldman had left Petaluma, California, as a forwarding address. The Internet confirmed both her address and phone number.

He punched in the number, and on the fourth ring, he heard, "This is Hannah Feldman."

Traveler briefly introduced himself and his reason for calling, and asked if they could meet face to face. She was hesitant, and although recognizing his name from his journalistic exploits, only agreed after Traveler had related key details about the Lincoln Memorial bombing.

He caught the first plane to San Francisco the next morning, then drove north to Petaluma. He found her house without trouble, a one-story bungalow on a quiet suburban street. Traveler greeted at the front door a woman whose face was lined and hair snow white, but he recognized the radiant smile from the photograph.

Now in her mid-seventies, she ushered Traveler into her neat but tiny living room, brightened by an impressive display of holiday decorations.

"I try to make the place as cheerful as possible, but the economy being what it is, you know..." she began.

Traveler replied graciously, "The economy has been such a disaster for so long, no one has been spared."

He accepted her offer of coffee and a slice of homemade banana cream pie. She left the room, returning with a tray of refreshments. Her hostess duties attended to, she sat down in an overstuffed chair and studied the photograph Traveler handed her.

"My, I haven't seen this picture in a long, long time. I can't believe I was ever that young." Traveler provided the pro forma protest that she brushed aside with a wry smile.

"Our parents brought my sister and me from Russia when we were quite small. Ours was a life of mere subsistence early on, trying to adjust to a new language and new surroundings. As for my nephew, I hadn't heard from or about him, I would guess, in almost thirty years.

"Out here, after awhile, you stop paying attention to what happens in the world. It's all such bad news. I neither watch television any more, nor read the paper. Thus, I was shocked to hear your description of the way he died."

Hannah listened to Traveler's further account of her nephew's life, registering little emotion; only her eyes widened from time to time as the recitation unfolded.

"Everything you've told me is so sad, so very sad. He was such an unfortunate boy, cursed you might say, from the beginning."

As it turned out, her story of Jaffe's younger years was even more astonishing than the events Traveler had just recounted.

❖

"When I was last in contact with him, a few years after he'd left high school, he had moved to Israel. You must understand that my nephew had suffered through a terrible early childhood. It's hard to imagine one worse for so small a child. His mother, my sister, had married a wonderful man, Samuel Jaffee, who died in a car crash when the boy was only a few years old.

"Her brother-in-law first provided consolation, then became his brother's replacement, in every sense of the word. They married within a year.

"There were three of them, you see, my sister, and her two sons, four years apart. And this man, who at first seemed like such a godsend after my sister was widowed, turned out to be as horrible as his brother was kind. He was truly demented.

"At first he was able to conceal his psychotic inner world from the rest of us, but little by little we began to see how brutally he was treating my sister and her boys. He was an unpredictable tyrant, and terrorized them, especially the boys.

"The elaborate set of regulations he established were straight out of a Kafka novel. There was no logic to these so-called rules, really, so the poor children never knew if they were abiding by them, or violating them.

"One of his more monstrous practices was to punish not the boy who had committed whatever the presumed offense was— but his sibling. A favorite punishment was to whip the boys, fierce whippings that left permanent scars. Several of us tried to intervene, but to no avail. His power over my sister, perverse as it was, was complete.

"My youngest nephew, Joshua, did find occasional respite from this nightmare. They lived on a farm, and he loved riding horses; I would guess it was his only means of escape."

Traveler dredged up lines, almost verbatim, he thought, from the long-forgotten poem that had been among the papers found in Jaffee's post office desk. He murmured to himself, "As a child, I envied the horses, with their muscled strength. If only I could once again ride those horses like the wind, to freedom."

Hannah continued, "There was an incident of incredible cruelty that finally forced the authorities to intercede." She stopped speaking, trembling slightly, her gaze fixed on the floor. Then, with a faraway voice, she told the tale.

"One day in late fall, their stepfather took the two boys fishing at a remote lake in the back country. They were in the middle of the lake in a small boat. It was one of those dreary, overcast fall days, with bone-chilling temperatures. They had been fishing without much luck, and very little conversation.

They were completely alone, this silent group of three, huddled in heavy raincoats. No one else was on the lake, or even visible on the distant shore.

"Suddenly, and without reason or provocation, my brother-in-law began a long, drawn-out harangue about the inequities of life. Most of what he said, as Joshua described it later, must have been stream-of-consciousness. He kept on ranting, speaking faster and louder. In a state of furious disgust, he hurled his pole, reel, line, and bait far out, beyond reach. 'This is useless!' he shouted. 'It's all useless!'

"Turning to the boys, in a low, contemptuous voice, he spat out, 'And you—*you* are useless.' He grabbed my older nephew and began beating him with an oar, finally knocking him overboard.

"Joshua watched, traumatized, taught to feel that he was to blame. He could only surmise that somehow this was his fault. No one ever determined the cause, if there was one—at least one that could be rationally understood."

Hannah drew in a breath, more like a gasp, really, and with a tremendous effort, continued.

"Then my brother-in-law calmly reattached the oar and methodically rowed away from the screaming child, knowing full well he couldn't swim. Can you imagine the scene, what that would do to the mind of a boy so young? A boy who felt that he was directly responsible for his brother's death?"

The question was rhetorical. Traveler merely nodded.

"Of course, this man—this animal—denied any culpability. He called it an accident. Joshua at first gave a true account of the incident to the authorities, but later refused to corroborate it in a legal document. He must have been terrified that he would become my brother-in-law's next target for retribution.

"My brother-in-law left town for good, and my sister lapsed into what the doctors diagnosed as a near-catatonic state. She became incapable of caring for her remaining son, so he was given over to me.

"Joshua seemed, in the next few years, to be coping, at least superficially. He did well in school. He even began collecting stamps, a hobby I could tell gave him some enjoyment. The centerpiece of his collection was his airmail stamps; he said they were dedicated to me, and I was deeply touched.

"He was never an outgoing boy, but that was understandable. There was always something distant or detached about him. After he left for Israel, for reasons I never really fathomed, other than any Jew's affinity for the Holy Land, we corresponded occasionally for awhile. I remember he said something about seeing a psychiatrist, which I was glad to hear, but I never learned the outcome.

"You know, I saved most of his letters. Maybe I can find the name of the doctor," she offered. Without waiting for Traveler to answer, she rose and left the room, returning with a faded envelope.

"Here's the one that refers to his therapy." She handed it to Traveler, who began reading avidly. In it, he found the name of Dr. Evelyn Westminster.

# CHAPTER THIRTY-FIVE

**Traveler left** Hannah Feldman's house knowing that the Chairman's people would provide whatever information existed about Dr. Westminster, and immediately received a complete profile, with instructions for contacting her in Israel. He called and told her about her former patient, and she was curious to hear more about the case. Fortunately, she said, she was about to leave Tel Aviv for New York, to attend a conference, and agreed to meet Traveler at her hotel in downtown Manhattan.

They met in her hotel lobby, and ascended a once-grand staircase to the bar and restaurant that had long ago been a gathering spot for the city's glitterati, but was now shuttered. "This was such an elegant hotel," Dr. Westminster remarked, as the two of them found a quiet sitting area. She was typecast to play a Freudian psychoanalyst. Her graying hair was pulled back into a tidy bun, and her pale blue eyes were framed by rimless glasses.

As they settled into a pair of shabby chairs, she offered Traveler a cigarette; he politely refused, so she lit it for herself. "It's a bad habit, I know, and I'm sure that it has some dreadful Freudian connotations, but I choose to suppress them," she said cheerfully.

The niceties dispensed with, she got right to the point. "Please show me the photographs and drawings you mentioned." He handed her the collection that had been amassed during the investigation.

"Yes," she confirmed, "this is the very same Joshua Jaffee I treated nearly twenty years ago, in 2005. He walked unannounced into my office and made an appointment; he apparently lived nearby, and, if nothing else, visiting me was convenient, I assume."

Traveler had come prepared with a series of questions, but Westminster was doing fine on her own.

"When I asked Joshua during initial sessions what had brought him to see me, he looked baffled. He said he wasn't sure, only that there were times when he felt fragmented, as if parts of his life kept disappearing. He had become aware that he would lose track of time, a few days, sometimes weeks. This was disquieting at the very least, as you can well imagine.

"In fact, Joshua claimed he wasn't even certain how he had gotten to Israel. After several sessions, I was convinced that his problem was neither amnesia nor garden-variety neurosis. You know, the typical patient's whining about some sort of injustice or deprivation. I'm sorry to be so politically incorrect. Maybe I've been a therapist too long."

Traveler was really beginning to like her.

"According to accepted psychoanalytic theory," she resumed, "I began trying to probe the early years of his life, but he volunteered no childhood recollections. The first ten years or so, at least on a conscious level, appeared a complete blank. Psychoanalysis is a process of assembling clues, however," she said, opening her briefcase and pulling out a folder full of papers. She thumbed through a few pages, and stopped abruptly.

"Here, for example, is an entry from one of our earlier sessions, referencing a dream he shared with me, which I had transcribed from a tape recording of that session. I'll read it exactly as he told it:

'He was a very good teacher. Somehow I knew that. If he had a friend, I was it. It must have been between classes when it happened. He was complaining of a terrible headache, and said he was afraid he might be having another attack. I wanted to call for help, but he insisted I just take him somewhere where he could lie down.

'The designated rest area in the high school was a room somewhere in the basement. He was staggering now, and leaning heavily on me. We had trouble finding the right room. Finally reaching it, he collapsed on the bed. He was sweating and wanted more air. I took off his shirt. You could see the welts all over his torso.

'I was getting scared. I yelled to a girl outside the room: Run to the office. Tell them to get an ambulance here immediately. She scampered off. He was getting worse and no help was arriving. I yelled to someone else in the hall: God damn it, go to the office and get help!

'The minutes kept ticking away. No help arrived. I jumped up and ran off to find help myself. Where the hell was the office located? I was lost. I couldn't find it. I was feeling absolute panic. What the hell would I say when I got to the office? This was insanity! I couldn't remember his name! What would I say: Ah, he's having an attack, you know, what's-his-name?'

Dr. Westminster closed the folder, took off her glasses, and met Traveler's stare. "A brief look into the unconscious, where many of our deepest feelings and motivations, often disguised, lie hidden. You note the patient's feelings of helplessness. A tragedy is taking place, and he feels powerless to deal with it."

Traveler was remembering Hannah Feldman's harrowing tale of her nephew—the whippings, bruises, that small boat on a cold fall afternoon. He imagined Joshua covering his ears, trying to drown out his brother's screams. As Dr. Westminster had phrased it, a tragedy was taking place and he felt powerless.

"The dream also speaks to a mystery of identities," Dr. Westminster said. "Who is the protagonist? Who is the endangered companion?"

They both fell silent, as if in accord; then Dr. Westminster stood up and announced, "You'll have to excuse me, but I'm running late." She agreed to meet again that evening, at the conclusion of the day's conference.

As Traveler and Westminster sat down to dinner that evening, the doctor began again. "The mind does a marvelous job of taking care of itself. It is remarkably self-protective. When confronted with thoughts or feelings with which it cannot cope, it compartmentalizes them. It sends them off to the brain's version of a Siberian gulag, but none of the information that our sensory system takes in is ever lost. It may get banished to far off places, but it's never permanently erased.

"I regard myself as an accomplished therapist, but how to reawaken ten lost years of a patient's life? I knew that if I were to succeed, the therapeutic process would be a lengthy one. Joshua wasn't prepared to make that kind of commitment, and before long ceased coming to see me."

In turn, Traveler gave her an overview of the Lincoln Memorial incident. He began with what Hannah Feldman had told him about Jaffee's youth, the first "missing" ten years, reviewed Jaffee's time spent as a car salesman and horse racing enthusiast in New York, and finally his tenure as a stamp-collecting postal employee in Washington.

Dr. Westminster said that as a rule she tried to avoid impulsive psychoanalytic pronouncements, but was choosing to make an exception in this case. "The airmail stamps obviously represent a lifelong affinity for his aunt, an airline employee, and changing his persona to someone with a carefree passion for horse racing must have been a great relief, just as riding had been for him as a child.

"Of course, we can still only speculate, but my patient's most accurate diagnosis may have been 'dissociative identity disorder,' a rare instance of multiple personality."

She stopped, lost in thought. Then it was as if the clouds parted. She looked at Traveler intently. "I don't believe I mentioned to you the nature of his work when I met him in Tel Aviv."

"No, you haven't," he said.

She spoke slowly. "He was working in road construction, learning demolitions, the use of explosives to carve paths through mountainous terrain." Almost as a non sequitur, she continued, "The mind is a wondrous mechanism, but under the most dreadful of circumstances, it is sometimes forced to resort to incongruent strategies.

"As he watched his brother's drowning, he would have thought, 'My act has caused this.' No small child's conscious mind can handle such a conclusion. It must be split off. That's the curious nature of the multiple personality. Rather than retreating into a psychotic state, which causes the individual's consciousness to totally withdraw from our reality, the mind creates several different conscious entities.

"A single body, then, is left inhabited by several personalities, each with a different world view. Joshua Jaffee, the postal employee who sought retribution against...let me call it an 'alien constituency'...was a personality seeking to rebalance the scales of justice."

"So what you're suggesting—" Traveler began.

Westminster cut him off impatiently. "I'm suggesting that Jaffee's several personalities were in conflict, and that one personality was determined to mete out justice against a counterpart, whom he blamed for his brother's drowning. That is, one personality arranged for the death of another—that would result in what we call suicide. Do not try to make sense of it. It is, after all, usually an irrational act.

"But I've speculated and suggested too much. You will need to excuse me. I have an early plane to catch in the morning. However, I'm sure the Chairman will make good use of this information."

# CHAPTER THIRTY-SIX

**As 2024 began**, Reverend Christian was welcomed back to the U.S. amid widespread euphoria, the delighted attraction in a ticker-tape parade through New York City, the likes of which had not been seen in decades. It was all orchestrated and financed by the Chairman.

Politicians and religious leaders applauded, even those who had previously condemned the excesses of the Reverend's evangelical movement. The Chairman's media blanketed the events with fawning coverage that all but assured that the Reverend would quickly become revered as a kind of warrior-saint; opinion polls showed his popularity skyrocketing, and he was now the most admired man in the nation.

The Chairman knew it was time, in this third decade of the twenty-first century, to seize the moment and announce the Reverend Christian and Conman as the presidential and vice presidential candidates of the newly formed New Politics party. The Chairman had complete and utter control over the two men. He had documented every illegal act and indiscretion they had ever committed. He could destroy them, and they knew it.

Sophia swung into action launching a New Politics media blitz. The presidential primaries were just beginning, and the campaign featured the Reverend Christian as the dynamic new leader America desperately needed. Conman played a supporting role, specifically targeting black and Hispanic voters.

The campaign message, which came directly from the Chairman, and Sophia's articulation of that message, were stunningly effective. Under the New Politics theme, "It Must Stop Now," Christian and Conman campaigned in perpetual motion, attending "town hall meetings." Their carefully constructed stump speech rarely varied, with only slight modifications now and then to address local issues.

"My fellow Americans," it began, "as we assemble here today, in 2024, the year of our Lord, we all know that we have reached a catastrophic impasse. We are at the precipice, looking into the abyss.

"We have watched conditions in our country deteriorate without interruption. Beyond our shores, we have watched the world's poor and disenfranchised shoulder the initial impact of unbearable environmental, population, and economic stress—resulting in outbreaks of plague, riot, and insurgency.

"Nations have failed, unleashing lawless, marauding hordes. We in the West have escaped much of this, have tried to look the other way, but we are on a similar path. It must stop now."

As this point, an arranged chant would slowly and softly begin to build within the crowd, "It must stop now. It must stop now."

"We are fast becoming our own failed state, as we battle inflation, unsustainable tax increases, dangerous and unparalleled levels of unemployment, the contamination of the very air we breathe, the water we drink. We watch roads and bridges crumbling, sometimes as if before our eyes, slums festering like cancerous lesions. We endure a terrible sense of personal danger—many of us feel it is unsafe to venture beyond our own homes.

"Can we let this go on any longer? No, it must stop now."

The crowd's refrain was louder this time. "It must stop now."

"We know what has brought us to this point of near-Armageddon. It is a bankrupt political system riddled with false promises, business-as-usual infighting, and gridlock; entrenched special interest groups struggle to protect their power base. We have been held captive by this failed system, immobilized, paralyzed. It must stop now."

"Stop now. Must stop now." The chant grew louder, the crowd more restive. "We are tired of being on the treadmill, going nowhere, trying to march up a down escalator. We are exhausted by lost hope, defeatism, pervasive impotence. It must stop now."

"Stop now, stop now, stop now—" the crowd roared.

"I will not deceive you, as others continue to do, pandering rather than putting forth hard choices. Those hard choices can no longer be ignored. That is why I am asking you to vote for new leadership—and to support the authorization of a new covenant, a new Constitution for our United States of America.

"I need not go into detail. The language of that new covenant is readily available on the Internet, national and local news. But the underlying premise is simple. We must have a stronger hand at the tiller. We can no longer allow our ship of state to run aground on the shoals of partisan bickering.

"We must empower a trusted president to *act alone*"…and these two words could not have been uttered more forcefully… "to act decisively in what he knows to be the best interests of our citizens. Our political stagnation must stop now."

"Now! Now! Now!"

"And let me conclude with perhaps the most hopeful news in decades. Both political parties have tried mightily to defeat its progress, and to conceal its existence, but since 2010 a consortium of our finest pharmaceutical companies has dedicated hundreds of scientists to perfecting a wondrous new medical breakthrough. Now, almost fifteen years later, they have finally perfected a harmless, non habit-forming curative analgesic that will be affordable to every man, woman, and child in this land of ours.

"It is akin—and I do not exaggerate—to discovering the fountain of youth, a reinvigorating miracle, a kind of elixir or tonic for our collective psychic malaise. It will help aid in giving us the strength to rebuild a sense of community. Because, my friends, ours is ultimately not just an issue of resources, but also one of spiritual rebirth.

"The core problem has been an overwhelming sense of despair. But the Lord has answered our supplications. He has given us the biochemical technology to help change that. I have heard His voice declare that America's past failures and weaknesses...must stop now!"

Then Reverend Christian or Conman, whoever delivered this stump speech, would plunge into the crowd to press the flesh, as the drumbeat of "it must stop now" rose in tempo, volume, and fervor.

The Chairman had brilliantly gauged the depth of the country's thirst for rebellion, even perhaps revolution. He knew history repeated itself. This was not the first time that a people had yearned for an all-powerful father figure, a shepherd who could be trusted to lead them out of the valley of the shadow of death. Mao, Stalin, Hitler had come before.

America's political left had been marginalized. It had talked the talk but never walked the walk. Its efforts to bridge the divide between the "two Americas"—those who had something, and those who had nothing—were always watered down, ultimately ineffectual. And now, as the Chairman had observed, those left with "something" had nearly vanished, and America was on the cusp of morphing into a single, almost nihilistic mob.

The hard core political right, now a tiny privileged class, still remained a formidable New Politics foe. Even though handicapped by incompetence and arrogance, its singular skill was in harnessing and manipulating free-floating anger. The political right believed that the country could be made to swallow any lie, the bigger the better. Never underestimate the stupidity of the American people, their leaders counseled—and they had repeatedly been proven correct.

The president, his staff, and conservative party leaders were blindsided when the Chairman launched the New Politics. They had assumed him to be an ally. Had he not most recently been the inspiration and brains behind the Islamic jihad ploy?

The Reverend Christian's emergence as a heroic figure had also been a surprise. The administration thoroughly ridiculed his announcement that he would not only run for president under the New Politics banner, but take Conman as his running mate. But the Chairman knew that the right's politics of division, of pitting one American against another, had finally run its course.

Having prematurely dismissed the New Politics fundamental strategy, building momentum through grass roots "town hall meetings," the administration late in the game began attacking these rallies with time-tested disruptive tactics. Conservative zealots were bused to each rally and entered meeting venues bearing scurrilous placards and spouting verbal abuse. Fistfights, even random gunfire increasingly occurred. It reached the point where neither Reverend Christian nor Conman dared attend some sessions. As the Chairman knew once more, such tactics were backfiring, reinforcing the New Politics contention that, "It must stop now."

❖

As the race neared its conclusion, the Chairman had a pair of extraordinary tricks up his sleeve, his *coup de grace*.

First, just weeks before the election, information was released that revealed the Lincoln Memorial conviction was not only a sham, but a sham engineered by the president himself. As Dr. Westminster had predicted, the Chairman surely did "make good use of the information" Traveler had uncovered.

Second, Sophia disseminated an allegation that the president's "black sheep" brother had gained access to the now-renowned second sheet of Inverted Jennies (which had escaped destruction in the Lincoln Memorial sting)—and that he had brokered a multi-million dollar deal with an anonymous Middle Eastern buyer.

Both allegations were hammer blows to old style politics. Voters angrily spurned these two acts as perfectly exemplifying the rotting system that had failed them for so long. The New Politics party won the 2024 election in a landslide.

A new Constitution was overwhelmingly approved, immediately ratified by individual states, granting the president unprecedented authority, and virtually dismantling the country's balance-of-power mechanisms. A consortium of pharmaceutical companies started delivering to drugstore shelves the "wondrous new medication" that the New Politics party had promised. It was highly cocaine-based.

The New Politics ideology spread rapidly through the North and South American continents, with populations worn down by economic misery happily ceding power in exchange for the pharmaceutical relief New Politics governments were providing.

As the dust was settling, two hundred and fifty years of inspired experiments in democracy were coming to an end. It was an era—a small deviation from eons of human tyranny—likely never to be seen again.

❖

A few weeks after the election, the Chairman was sitting alone, as he always did in his darkened room, contemplating the fishing boat incident that had been the origin of Joshua Jaffee's lifelong turmoil—the revelation of which had helped turn the tide in the U.S. presidential race.

"And to think that the death blow was a fish story," he gloated, as he donned an Alfred E. Neuman mask of his own design. It depicted Alfred E. as Jesus, when he said to two of his disciples, "Come ye after me, and I will make you to become fishers of men."

The Chairman giggled as he slipped it on, crying rapturously, "I am the supreme fisher of men, king of kings. Look on my works, ye mighty and despair!"

# CHAPTER THIRTY-SEVEN

**A month after** the election, Traveler and Sophia were back in Havana, enjoying the final days of the year. They had discharged their duties to the Chairman, and were relieved to finally escape from the maelstrom of his convoluted world.

As Traveler had done so often in the past, he went fishing with Adolfo; they followed their usual routine and met early at the docks.

The boat left the harbor, and the two men casually held their rods until several miles offshore, when the lines were run out. Adolfo now turned to Traveler. "Enjoying yourself?" he asked.

"I'm feeling well, mostly good days."

"I would imagine that has a lot to do with Sophia. She's a lovely woman."

The boat began a wide turn, as the skipper started an extended pass over the stretch of water they would begin the day trolling.

It was not long before Traveler felt a mighty tug at his line. Pulling his pole up sharply, he attempted to set the hook. The line began to run out, and he let the fish try to free itself without allowing too much slack to form. Then, tightening the line, he reeled in quickly whenever the fish grew weary or turned towards the boat.

Traveler patiently brought the fish nearer, as the marlin

periodically broke the water's surface with dramatic leaps. Traveler drew the fish closer and closer to the boat, but with one final, desperate surge, the marlin thrust its bill skyward, and shook its head. The two men watched as the lure flew loose, and the fish, shining in the sun, returned to the sea.

"You're free, Joshua," Adolfo said inexplicably, and then tilting his head towards a large canvas bag secured in the bow, "You haven't asked about that."

"I figured you would get to it when you were ready," Traveler said.

"Most of the money has been wired to your account, but I thought you might like a little pocket change. You and Sophia are very, very wealthy. But tell me, how did you gain possession of the stamps? I thought they had been reduced to ashes in the African ambassador's office."

"So it was reported," said Traveler. "Actually, Malika and Sophia, apprehensive about the arranged transaction, had substituted a near-perfect copy of the rediscovered pane. After making certain the five hundred million dollars was in their possession, they fully intended to deliver the genuine pane to the ambassador.

"They knew that to double-cross anyone with the ability to pay the amount of money in question—would mean their death sentence."

"All's well that ends well, I guess," Adolfo shrugged. "For me it has meant that my Israeli citizenship will be coming through soon. There aren't many habitable places left on this poor old planet of ours, and God knows Israel is hardly one of them, but I am grateful nonetheless. I'll be able to die and be buried in my ancestral homeland—and it could not have happened without your help."

"So the buyer was satisfied with the stamps?"

"He could not have been more pleased. His grandfather was a fighter pilot hero of the Six Day War, almost sixty years ago—when the Jews overwhelmed the Arabs, mainly thanks to the Israeli air force. The grandson, an ardent stamp collector and one of the Middle East's richest men, idolized his grandfather; thus the nucleus of his collection is airmails."

"A strange twist of fate," Traveler replied. "Joshua Jaffee and our buyer sharing a passion for airmail stamps."

Changing the subject, Adolfo asked in jest, "Will you tithe away some of your financial windfall?"

Gesturing towards the canvas bag, Traveler answered, "Allah will certainly be getting his fair share. Sophia and Malika will see to that."

Adolfo signaled to the skipper to return to Havana harbor. The lines were pulled in, and the two men prepared for a homecoming, one in another country, the other with the woman he loved.

❖

Several days later, as dusk approached, Traveler and Sophia left their hotel, heading towards old Havana. They walked along a strip of beach that hugs the Gulf of Mexico, ending at Havana Bay.

Sophia was in a sprightly mood; she had absorbed the energy that seems to infuse Latin countries, no matter how poor, and she was sharing it with the man she adored. As the couple ambled along, she would occasionally race ahead, tease him to follow, and skip lightly back.

He had brought his cane, in case he grew tired, and they walked eastwards, stopping periodically for a stunning view of the majestic Castillo de Morro.

Sophia watched the seabirds swoop and circle above the harbor. Large groups would break up into smaller clusters, as if following some command only they could hear.

She drew close to Traveler, entwining her fingers in his, and began to swing their arms back and forth like children, perhaps prompted by the youngsters frolicking in the shallow water along the shore.

The couple passed a motley handful of musicians, enthusiastically rapping out a rhythmic song with tambourines, castanets, and flutes. Sophia began to sway and twirl to the hypnotic sound, trying to coax a reluctant Traveler to join her in a playful, whirling dance.

They soon found themselves inadvertently on a stretch of shoreline concealed from view by a grove of palm trees. A single figure was sitting on the sand, an old man, turbaned in the

Middle Eastern style, tending a small fire as a chill wind had begun to blow from the north.

As he piled dried palm fronds on the fire, Sophia suddenly grabbed the stem of a flaming branch from the fire, holding it in one hand as she ran to the sea's edge, scooped up a handful of water in her other hand, and raced away into the distance.

Traveler gazed after her with puzzled delight. "She is a most spiritual woman," the turbaned man said. As Traveler turned towards him, he continued, "Perhaps, sir, you do not know about the woman in Sufi legend who, in one of her more famous stories, runs down a path with water in one hand and fire in the other. According to lore, it speaks to the art of practicing attached detachment."

"I'm not sure I follow," Traveler said.

The man laughed softly. "Said another way, it is feeling deeply attached while also remaining apart. The Sufis believe this is a road to spiritual enlightenment. I'm afraid that is the best explanation I can make."

Traveler smiled. "And how has one filled with so much wisdom come to be sitting on the shore of Havana's bay, before a fire?" he asked the old man.

"That, sir, is a long story, and your companion awaits you."

To catch up with Sophia, Traveler found he was able to move more quickly than he had in years, and after he rejoined her, they continued their stroll hand-in-hand. With evening upon them, the sky slowly darkened, with the wind from the north perhaps presaging an impending storm; they reached the outskirts of Havana's old town, and stopped to take a close view of El Morro.

El Morro had been the site of fierce warfare, and the bloodiest battle had taken place when the British seized the fort in the late 1700s, leaving nearly a thousand Spanish soldiers captured, wounded, or dead. Traveler knew the history intimately, and as he gazed upon the old fort, he thought he heard the faint sounds of artillery, and smelled a whiff of gun smoke. He knew the signs all too well—a mild flashback to Bosnia, likely provoked as the fort loomed larger.

Traveler forced himself to take deep, slow breaths. Sophia turned to him, with concern. He drew her close; she said nothing, just held him for a few moments, and the memory passed.

Traveler reflected on the extraordinary experience he and Sophia had recently shared. What was it in life that he had wished to find? Would there be an assured refuge? He still wasn't certain, but he felt closer to the answers than ever before.

Traveler had the sensation of once again arriving at a crossroads, and that he was moving in what was for him a direction unfamiliar, a path less taken. He walked to the shoreline with Sophia, and taking his cane, threw it far out into the water. Then they turned, and continued their journey together up the beach.